Bolan primed a frag grenade, then tossed the bomb

He waited for the blast, and when it came he made his move, crawling toward the club's rear exit while all hell broke loose behind him. He reached the door, barged through it and jumped to his feet.

The Triad gunners were close behind him, closing fast.

The man who stepped in front of the Executioner as he turned out of the alley was Caucasian. The pistol in his hand was cocked and aimed past the warrior, toward the back door of the club.

"Watch out!" the stranger snapped, unloading four quick rounds almost before the words had passed his lips.

Downrange, the first Triad hardman to clear the doorway went down on his back. The next shooter, a step or two behind him, clutched his side and toppled several trash cans as he fell.

A burst from Bolan's Uzi drove the others back inside—a temporary respite from the chase. The Executioner's savior made no attempt to stop him as he turned back from the club and headed toward Pender Street.

MACK BOLAN ®

The Executioner

DON PENDLETON'S
THE EXECUTIONER®
FIRE LASH

THE RED DRAGON TRILOGY
BOOK I

FIRE LASH

A GOLD EAGLE BOOK FROM
WORLDWIDE.

TORONTO • NEW YORK • LONDON
AMSTERDAM • PARIS • SYDNEY • HAMBURG
STOCKHOLM • ATHENS • TOKYO • MILAN
MADRID • WARSAW • BUDAPEST • AUCKLAND

First edition June 1996
ISBN 0-373-64210-5

Special thanks and acknowledgment to
Mike Newton for his contribution to this work.

FIRE LASH

There is no need to fear the strong. All one needs is to know the method of overcoming them. There is special jujitsu for every strong man.

—Yevgeny Yevtushenko

The expansion of corrupt power is a dangerous thing for humankind, but it doesn't need to happen unopposed. If history has taught us anything, we must remember where to draw the line and make a stand.

—Mack Bolan

For Chief Warrant Officer David Hilemon and Pilot Bobby Hall,
U.S. Army. God keep.

PROLOGUE

Macau

If he could only reach the harbor, Chan decided, he would have a fighting chance to stay alive. Not much, perhaps, but anything was better than remaining in his cramped hotel room or the bar downstairs and waiting for the Dragon to come hunting him.

That was suicide, and Chan hadn't survived this long, against such overwhelming odds, by giving up when things got tough.

He was a fighter, born and raised in a tradition of defiance to the hostile world around him. One of thirteen children, Chan could easily have wound up as a lowly fisherman, or working in a sweatshop, but his parents had invested him with strength that went beyond the physical, an inner toughness that allowed him to prevail when other men gave up and let their enemies walk over them as if they were pathetic doormats, woven out of straw. Chan had prevailed in every struggle up to this point in his life, and even though he recognized the odds against him now, he didn't have it in him to surrender.

The harbor was his hope. If he could reach the ferry, he had a decent shot at reaching Hong Kong while his enemies were still disorganized. They might be waiting for him at the dock, in which case Chan could try to commandeer a private craft and slip away unseen.

Whatever happened, he would have a better chance of living through the night if he could put Macau behind him. He had friends in Hong Kong who would help him, hide him from his enemies.

But the Dragon's reach was long, his talons sharp and venomous. Chan's friends weren't invincible. By seeking help from them, he placed their lives in danger, but they understood the risks involved. Chan's allies shared his passion and commitment. They would sacrifice themselves, if need be, to defeat the common enemy.

It had begun to drizzle, and Chan was miserable in the alley, strewn with garbage, where he stood and watched the traffic flowing past him, almost close enough to touch. He was a half mile from the harbor, but it might as well have been located on the dark side of the moon.

The Dragon would be sniffing after him already, scouring the crowded streets to find his scent. If he didn't move quickly, it would be too late.

Chan watched three taxis pass him, headed toward the harbor. He could flag down the next one, try to pick out a driver who wasn't beholden to his enemy, but there was too much risk in that. Chan's first mistake would be his last, a quick detour into darkness, grim assassins waiting for him when the taxi stopped.

He would be better off on foot.

In decent weather, with no one chasing him, he could have made the trek in twenty minutes. This night was different, though. Chan had to watch his step, beware of strangers, shadows, anything at all. The Dragon wore a thousand faces, but they shared a common trait—each one was deadly, a potential killer. Any one of them could stop Chan cold, wipe out a year's hard work and keep the crucial information he possessed from getting to the proper hands.

It would be worth his life, perhaps, to know that he had slowed the Dragon a bit, derailed the master plan.

But first he had to reach Hong Kong alive, and he wouldn't accomplish that by staying where he was.

Chan left the alley, moving cautiously. The automatic pistol in the right-hand pocket of his raincoat didn't make him feel secure.

He'd spent twelve months among the Dragon's servants before he knew what they were up to. Chan also knew of their fanatical devotion to the cause, the suicidal risks that any one of them would take to punish treason in the ranks. His days—no, *hours*—would be numbered in Macau, perhaps in Hong Kong, too. Once he reported in, though, Chan could travel anywhere, pick out a new identity and place himself beyond the Dragon's reach.

If such a thing was possible.

He could only imagine what awaited him if he was brought to book for spying on the Dragon, feeding information back to the authorities.

He covered half a block before the sniper found him. Movement saved his life, but only just. The bullet came from nowhere, silenced, chipping masonry so close to Chan that brick dust settled in his hair like dandruff, jagged splinters drawing blood beneath one eye.

Chan bolted, charging into traffic, running with his arms crossed overhead as if the bullets could be kept at bay like raindrops. He zigzagged through the stream of taxis, compacts, rented mokes and pedicabs. A looming bus passed close enough to stagger him, and Chan imagined that he heard a bullet strike the massive vehicle.

He reached the far side of the street and ducked around the corner, jostling strangers when they failed to clear the way. A shot struck glass somewhere behind him, and he heard a woman's startled cry of pain before he cleared the target zone.

The grim, one-sided battle had been joined. It could have been coincidence, but Chan had learned enough about the Dragon to believe an army would be tracking him by now.

The spotters would have been staked out at intervals around his living quarters, and he had no doubt the sniper would be spreading an alarm, reporting the direction of Chan's flight, describing what he wore.

Evasive action was the key. A reeking alley opened on his left, and Chan ducked into it. He had to watch his step here, where the streetlights didn't reach, for there was garbage underfoot and he couldn't afford a twisted ankle now, when speed was everything.

Chan slowed before he reached the alley's exit, stuck his head out in the clear and pulled it back again. No gunshots. Were they lying back and waiting for him to emerge, where they would have a better shot? Chan knew he had to take the chance, or else stay where he was and wait for them to take him.

He made his move, using every bit of self-restraint to keep from running wildly down the sidewalk. No one spared a second glance for Chan as he emerged from the dark alley. He was just another passerby, one of 370,000 people crammed into six square miles of Portuguese territory.

On impulse, Chan stopped short, stepped to the curb and flagged down a pedicab. He didn't haggle over price, a circumstance that made the young driver hesitate. The first price he had quoted for a straight run to the docks was several dollars high, and he had been prepared to bargain down. Chan's swift acceptance of the fare made him suspicious, but his apprehension faded after Chan stuffed the money into his pocket, stepped around behind him and settled in the cab's small seat.

"Let's go! I'm in a hurry!"

"Yes, sir!"

It was a risk, Chan knew, but this man didn't seem to have the Dragon's look about him. If they deviated from the normal course or made an unexpected stop, Chan was prepared to use his pistol, and the driver would be first to die.

Chan turned up the collar of his raincoat and ducked his head, using the umbrella that came with the pedicab to help conceal his face from passersby. It was a poor disguise, and no protection whatsoever from a bullet, but he had no other options at the moment. Chan had made his judgment call in haste, and he was on his way to the docks.

In fact, he changed his mind when they were still a few blocks from the harbor, shouting for the young man to pull over. His driver was confused and started to object, afraid that he would have to give some of the money back, when Chan bailed out and waved him off, proceeding toward the docks on foot.

That way, at least he had a chance of spotting any lookouts who were waiting for him at the ferry slip, before they saw him. It wasn't a great plan, granted, but he had to make up the refinements as he went along.

He kept one hand inside his pocket, wrapped around the automatic pistol, as he finally approached the waterfront. The rain was letting up, and he could smell the ocean, see the lights of Hong Kong.

He stood in shadow, checking out the lighted ferry slip. They were already loading for the midnight run, cars vanishing into the ferry's open maw, pedestrians lined up to board like patrons at a theater. He scanned the parking lot, his sweep arrested by the long black limousine that stood to one side, waiting like a predator. It radiated menace, bristling the short hairs on Chan's nape.

He couldn't swear that servants of the Dragon were inside the car. Dark tinted windows hid the occupants from view, and it could just as well be owned by any of a thousand well-heeled businessmen... But why, in that case, would the limousine be parked on the sidelines, rather than in line to board the ferry? Was it logical to think that someone rich would leave his vehicle behind and try to walk around Hong Kong, or relegate himself to taxis when he had a limousine on call?

It was enough to put Chan off, but he wasn't done yet. Besides the ferry, there were hydrofoils and jetfoils running back and forth from Hong Kong to Macau, along with private craft that could be rented by the hour. Chan would make it yet, unless his adversaries had each pier and slip staked out.

He wandered south, the ferry at his back, in search of someone who would take him over to the island with no questions asked. Chan had no fear that anyone he met would sell him out to the police. That kind of thing was frowned upon along the waterfront, and while the law would certainly have spies in the vicinity, their function was to gather information and report at leisure, not to intercept a desperate fugitive.

Chan's greatest risk from the police, in any case, would be the danger of encountering patrolmen or detectives who were paid off by the Dragon. Hong Kong had no corner on corruption when it came to the police. A fair percentage of them always had their hands out in Macau, as well. It was a standard cost of doing business on the wrong side of the law—a kind of tax on crime—and those who took the Dragon's money found themselves on call for special favors, as the need arose.

He spied a young man just emerging from the shadows of a warehouse, twenty yards in front of him, proceeding toward the nearest pier. A boat was waiting for him there. Not new, but it seemed in decent shape, more powerful than any of the private craft one found along the waterfront. If Chan could strike a bargain with the stranger, he would have a swifter and more comfortable trip than if he had to bribe some family for a lift aboard their crowded junk. And, if the young man wouldn't deal, Chan had the pistol to persuade him. Any charges could be dealt with by his contacts on the other side, once they considered his report and realized its value.

They would help him get away, no doubt about it.

What else could they do?

Chan crossed the twenty yards of asphalt, calling out to the young man before he reached the pier, not wanting to alarm him. As it was, the young man didn't seem surprised. He stood at ease, watched Chan approach. If there was anything about him that seemed nervous, it was his eyes, the way his gaze kept flicking left and right.

Across Chan's shoulder.

By the time Chan recognized his peril, it was already too late. The young man took off running, while Chan turned back to face the warehouse, reaching for his automatic.

Two men emerged from the shadows, thirty-five or forty feet between them. In the semidarkness, Chan initially mistook them both for hunchbacks, then he realized that they were wearing packs or tanks of some kind on their backs. Each held a stubby weapon, something like a spray gun, linked by drooping hoses to the packs they wore.

Chan recognized the weapons and felt his stomach twisting in a knot as it came to him that there was no escape. He drew the automatic from his pocket and thumbed the hammer back.

Too late.

Twin streams of fire erupted from the flamethrowers his adversaries held, converging on their human target, crossing, merging into one. Chan screamed once, then the blazing heat sucked air out of his lungs and seared his larynx shut. He staggered blindly in a circle, lurching toward the water as bright flames devoured his clothing, flesh and muscle, eating toward the bone. With any luck, he might have been dead by the time he toppled over, plunging into darkness like a comet from the heavens, splashing down amid a cloud of steam.

Chan's executioners switched off their weapons, watching from a distance as the pool of jellied gasoline where Chan had stood continued burning, asphalt bubbling into molten tar. They didn't need to check their handiwork, and remained immobile as another pair of men emerged from the surrounding shadows.

Cheung Kuo was smiling as he stepped around the pool of fire and followed blazing footsteps to the water's edge. Below him, near the dock, a blackened scarecrow floated facedown on the brackish tide. Kuo's grim companion, Edward Wong, scowled at the stench of burning flesh.

"You think my methods are excessive, Wong?"

The scowler shrugged. "I would have simply shot the man."

"But this way, our friend Chan will serve as an example of the Dragon's wrath. It is poetic, don't you think?"

"If you say so."

"I do, indeed. Poetic justice. You should cultivate imagination, Edward. It would do you good."

"I'll try my best," Wong replied.

"Come, now. We've tarried long enough. There's work remaining to be done."

Wong turned and followed the Red Dragon back into the shadows, two assassins bringing up the rear. It would be daylight in a few more hours, and he could forget about this night.

The Dragon's second-in-command was looking forward to a bold new day.

San Francisco

Dense fog was stealing over San Francisco as Mack Bolan drove his rented Chrysler Concorde west on Washington, from the Embarcadero. When he checked the rearview mirror, he could see it chasing him, like smoke from an advancing brushfire, blotting out the streetlights, neon and pedestrians. He was reminded of a story he'd once read while taking a little R & R, where an eerie mist descended upon a small town in New England, bringing prehistoric carnivores and God knew what else to hunt the panicked citizens.

It crossed his mind that there were monsters in this creeping fog, as well, but they were man-size, strictly modern predators. And when the fog had settled in this night, the monsters would discover *they* were being hunted for a change.

The U.S. Customs building loomed on Bolan's right, then vanished after he had covered half a block. The fog was perfect. He couldn't have hoped for better if he was allowed to pick the weather from a cosmic menu of his own design. Most times a soldier had to tolerate the weather, make the best of what he couldn't change, but every now and then he caught a break.

Crossing over Kearny, the 600 block of Washington, he felt the change from mainstream San Francisco into Chinatown. The street signs said it all, if you could see them through the fog, along with shop fronts decorated in the Old World style. The butchers hung ducks and chickens in their windows, plucked and dangling by their necks like victims of some cartoon lynching. Apothecaries specialized in remedies the FDA had never heard of, much less rubber-stamped as medicine: all kinds of roots and herbs, with the occasional concoction from endangered species thrown in for variety. Displays in pawnshop windows ran toward fans and ornate razors, hand-carved ivory and jade.

There was a good chance that many of the men or women passing on the street were in the States illegally, pieces of human cargo smuggled from Hong Kong to Amsterdam, Vancouver, Mexico—and on from there to settle in the Promised Land. Most of them came in peace, with honorable motives, refugees from poverty and persecution on the Chinese mainland, but their ranks included spies and mercenary criminals, as well. Some who couldn't afford the price of passage carried drugs or other contraband to pay their way. Without exception, the illegal immigrants were easy prey to those who recognized their status and were willing to apply strategic pressure as the need arose.

One such was Sammy Ng, the self-styled Lord of Chinatown. A fifth-generation American, descended from miners and railway laborers, Ng sprang from pioneer stock as surely as any blue-blooded descendant of *Mayflower* Pilgrims. His ancestors were from the East, and they had landed on a different coast, but they had suffered hardship all the same—more so than many early settlers of New England, with the anti-Chinese riots and congressional Exclusion Acts that had endured through the latter half of the nineteenth century.

Small wonder some of them had banded into Tongs, for self-defense and mutual assistance on the wild frontier. It was no mystery at all how certain members of the Tongs—and, later, whole organizations—had drifted into criminal activity as an alternative to dying in the mines or sweating eighteen-hour days to clean the white man's laundry. It was easier and much more profitable to sell opium, set up a makeshift gambling house or run a string of prostitutes. In San Francisco and Los Angeles, the Tongs were fighting over turf before the first scouts from the Mafia set sail from Sicily to look for opportunities around New Orleans and New York.

Times changed, but easy money always had the same appeal, and human predators were rarely known to change their stripes. The Tongs existed at two vastly different levels. A few were public-service groups, benevolent in the extreme, no more suspicious than the Shriners, Elks or Lions club. Some others were controlled by the elusive Chinese syndicates called Triads, recognized by law enforcement as the largest and most ruthless criminal "families" on earth. By 1985, known members of the Chinese Triads had outnumbered mafiosi by an estimated twenty-five to one, worldwide, and there had been no cutbacks to the payroll since that time. Their major stock-in-trade was heroin— "China white" imported from the Golden Triangle of Southeast Asia—but traffic in illegal immigrants had rivaled drugs in recent years, as new oppressive measures from Beijing encouraged thousands to desert their homeland for a safer climate.

With an estimated 100,000 mainland Chinese illegally entering the United States each year, at an average of $15,000 per head to the smugglers, it was a new world of profit for the Triads. Better yet, since smugglers collected only $1,000 or so on departure, frightened newcomers were left to work off the bulk of their debt in America, through sweatshop labor, prostitution or other forms of extortion. The price of refusal was a phone call to Immigration and a one-way ticket home to face the wrath of Communist authorities.

In San Francisco, Chinatown was bounded on the south by California Street, by Broadway on the north; its demarcation lines on east and west were Kearny Street and Taylor Street, respectively. It was a different world within those forty-nine square city blocks, sometimes inscrutable to whites. But Bolan knew enough of what went on in Asian minds to recognize that their society included predators and prey, like any other grouping of humankind.

His target, on this foggy evening, was a combination gambling hall and cutting plant for heroin that Sammy Ng maintained on Hangah Street. Bolan passed a playground and Pagoda Street, then, with Hangah up ahead, he turned left onto Brooklyn, found a place to park and locked his rental car.

In other circumstances, the Executioner would have dressed to kill: the combat blacksuit, military webbing, war paint blacking out his face and hands. This night, in these surroundings, though, he had to compromise. A white man strolling into Chinatown might raise some eyebrows, but it happened all the time. Some came in search of bargains, Chinese meals, vacation snapshots; others spent their cash on women, drugs and favors purchased from the Triads. Either way, a white man in a business suit and raincoat would be less conspicuous than one in paramilitary garb who went in laden down with weapons and explosives.

Which wasn't to say that Bolan went unarmed. He wore the usual Beretta 93-R automatic pistol with its custom silencer beneath his left arm, in a fast-draw rig. Below his right arm, riding swivel leather, was an Uzi submachine gun, also silenced, with a folding metal stock. The inner pockets of his raincoat carried extra magazines, while smoke and fragmentation grenades were clipped onto his belt. A razor-edged stiletto and piano-wire garrote completed the ensemble, leaving Bolan able to defend himself in any situation short of aerial bombardment or a clash with armored vehicles.

He had the address memorized, walked past it in the fog and satisfied himself that there were no troops posted on the street. Illegal operations were protected just the same in Chinatown as anywhere on earth, with bribes and guns, but no external sentries were considered necessary in this part of San Francisco, when the owner's name was Sammy Ng. His name alone would frighten most Chinese—and many whites—enough to keep potential thieves and saboteurs away.

But names wouldn't dissuade the Executioner.

He turned into a pitch-black alley, found the fire escape by feel, drew down the well-oiled ladder and started climbing toward his target.

THE TURNOUT for the Lung Cheung Club was always small on Wednesday nights. It was a mystery to Billy Lee, but there you had it, carved in stone, a fact of life that no one could explain. Six nights a week the club was open, all but Sundays, and they hadn't shown a decent take on Wednesday nights since Lee started working there two years earlier.

Go figure.

Lung cheung translated into "happy dragon," and the image always brought a smile to Lee's face. To him, a dragon was the kick-ass monster from your wildest nightmares, scarfing people down like popcorn after they were roasted with its fiery breath. The very notion of a *happy* dragon was incongruous; it went against the grain.

Still, with a gambling club, you had to give the suckers cause for optimism, let them cling to feeble hope while they watched hard-earned money slipping through their hands. Next time the cards were dealt or dice were rolled, the dragon might be smiling. Lady Luck might snuggle up and stay awhile.

Fat chance.

It didn't really matter if the club showed red ink once a week, of course, because the cutting plant upstairs was always in the black. Lee didn't know what Sammy Ng was paying these days for his uncut China white, but after it was stepped on ten or fifteen times, his profit margin shot straight through the roof and into orbit. All the tabloid TV shows were running spots about how heroin had staged a comeback in the States, against cocaine, but Lee could have told them that a year before they started airing breathless exposés. He knew it by the volume Ng was moving through the mill upstairs—and that was only one of a half-dozen cutting plants in Chinatown.

The cutting plant had soldiers of its own, but Lee had to go upstairs and check the action two or three times a night, to satisfy his boss that everything was cool. A certain paranoia came along with running smack, he realized, and trust was constantly in short supply, despite the fierce, long-winded oaths each member of the Triad took upon initiation to the brotherhood. It was the reason workers in the cutting plant, both men and women, stripped to shorts or panties when they clocked in for their shift and worked the whole time almost naked—so they couldn't try to hide an ounce or two for private use or sale.

Lee hated going upstairs to the plant because he had to put on the mask, covering his nose and mouth to keep from breathing any dust and picking up a habit on the sly. The first few times, it was a trip to see the women working topless, but their eyes were dead between the shower caps and masks they wore, like zombies. Tits were nothing special in an atmosphere like that. If anything, he was turned off.

Lee tried to focus on his job downstairs. Except for Wednesday nights, they always had some kind of action going at the club. A handful of the players did all right, encouraging the others to bet more and more, in hopes of riding on their coattails. Some of them were shills, of course, while others caught a real-life lucky streak and went home with an extra grand or two to brag about. It didn't hurt to have some winners out there, advertising for the club by word of mouth, as long as most of those who visited the Happy Dragon walked out with empty pockets.

It was still a business, after all, and anybody looking for a handout ought to try the local rescue mission.

Lee checked his watch and frowned. Another thirty minutes, give or take, and he would have to go upstairs again. It was a total waste of time, in his opinion, but he didn't feel like telling that to Sammy Ng. Defiance of the red pole was a shortcut to career stagnation—maybe worse—and Billy Lee wouldn't make *that* mistake if he could help it.

It was no big deal, for God's sake—walk upstairs and put on the mask, check out the zombies and ask their foreman how it was going; nod approvingly when he replied, "No problem, everything okay."

How simple could it be?

Lee had his right foot on the bottom step, already reaching in his pocket for the mask, when an explosion rocked the building. He staggered and almost lost his balance, throwing out an arm to brace himself against the nearest wall. Dust filtered from the ceiling, and he heard the handful of determined Wednesday gamblers bolting from their tables, babbling like a bunch of frightened children as they headed for the exit.

The gunner started up the stairs again, remembering to tie his mask in place before he reached inside his jacket for his pistol. He told himself it was some kind of accident and hoped the zombies could contain it. If they had to call the fire department, there would be no end of questions. Sammy Ng would have to spread all kinds of bribes around, and even then it might not be enough to keep the lid on.

At least it wasn't one of Lee's busy nights. He could be thankful for small favors, keep his fingers crossed that it was nothing that would bring the law around. If people had been hurt upstairs, then he would have to clean them up and drive them to the hospital—or, better yet, send out for one of his boss's private doctors to come to treat them on the spot. No ambulance, with broadcasts on the two-way radio that anyone could hear if he or she was tuned in to the proper frequency.

Suppose it wasn't an accident?

The thought raised bristles on his nape, and Billy Lee pulled out his automatic, rushing up the stairs to find out what the hell was going on.

BOLAN HESITATED on the landing of the fire escape, just long enough to slip on his mask and goggles. He had barged into cutting plants before and knew the kind of atmosphere he could expect. The gauze and goggles would protect him to a point, and in the absence of a proper gas mask they would have to do, but it wouldn't be in his own best interest to prolong the action, once he put the ball in play. Aside from simple breathing, there were hostile guns to think about, and Bolan had to guess that reinforcements for the standing crew would be available, once the alarm was raised.

The windowpanes had been painted solid black, a careful job to keep the inner light from shining through and to frustrate any prying eyes on the outside. The fact that only one floor had been so treated confirmed the information from Bolan's street informant, reassuring the soldier that he had the proper target in his sights. From this point on, each move he made would be destructive, costing lives, and he had no desire to burst in on a common sweatshop or a meeting of a Chinese social club.

He palmed a frag grenade, backed down the metal staircase several steps to give himself some clearance, yanked the safety pin and made the pitch. Glass shattered, spilling light into the fog, as Bolan threw himself facedown against the metal steps.

The greater part of the explosion was contained inside brick walls, but there was still enough left over to clear half a dozen windows, jagged shards of painted glass erupting from the windowframes like shrapnel, raining on Bolan, cutting crazy abstract patterns in the fog.

The Executioner was up and moving well before the echo of the blast had ceased reverberating. He went in behind the Uzi, through a swirling cloud of smoke and million-dollar dust that would have dropped a rhino in its tracks without the proper breathing apparatus.

Those assigned to work the plant were wearing masks, of course, but little else. The briefs they wore on the production line gave no protection whatsoever against shrapnel and bullets. Their watchdogs were no better prepared for an assault than those assigned to cut the heroin and package it for resale on the street. In theory they were soldiers, but the soft life undermined preparedness, and none of them had ever counted on a raider coming through the window, leading with explosives.

Half a dozen bodies were sprawled on the floor as Bolan entered, most of them near-naked drones from the production line, some of them leaking life from shrapnel wounds, others stunned or knocked unconscious by the blast. A couple of the casualties were female, but he spared no sympathy for them because of gender. They were in the business of dispensing misery and death to earn their daily bread. What goes around—

A soldier came into his field of vision from the left, a lurching shadow, squeezing off two pistol shots at nothing, more in the direction of the shattered windows than toward Bolan. He was dazed, disoriented, but there was no point allowing him to get his second wind. The Uzi stuttered through its custom silencer, three rounds exploding through the shooter's chest and dropping him amid the ruins of the plant's production line.

Another gun went off to Bolan's right, and he could feel the bullet whisper past his face. The Uzi spit back—three, four, five rounds at a range of twenty feet—and Bolan saw his target stagger, reeling from the impact, going down.

Two more shadow shapes came at him from the swirling murk. Both had pistols drawn, but neither one was firing yet, eyes squinting as they tried to find a proper target. Bolan didn't let them have the chance, his submachine gun stitching them from left to right and back again, 9 mm manglers ripping flesh and fabric, dropping both men in their tracks.

He scanned the room again, ignoring a couple of the stunned or wounded drones who were endeavoring to stand. Unarmed and half-blind, they posed no threat to Bolan. Moving rapidly across the smoky battlefield, he reached the only door and opened it in time to meet a young man with a pistol halfway up the stairs.

Surprise was written on the Asian gunner's face, despite the mask of gauze he wore. He tried to raise his pistol, but his hand was trembling with a mixture of amazement, shock and fear. The guy was shouting something in Chinese when Bolan shot him, hot rounds ripping blowholes in his chest, releasing spouts of crimson as the young man tumbled backward, descending the staircase in an awkward somersault. He landed in a heap and didn't move again.

Downstairs, the gambling club was bedlam, shouts of panic wafting up from men the Executioner couldn't see. There could be other guns down there for all he knew, and while the narrow staircase offered him a fair defensive posture, Bolan didn't have the time to hang around and fight a long pitched battle at the Lung Cheung Club.

Instead, he took a smoke grenade, released the pin and lobbed the can down the stairs, beyond the fallen gunner's body. It was spewing clouds of choking fumes before it wobbled out of sight, and Bolan followed with a second smoker to maximize confusion for the troops downstairs.

Bolan returned to the cutting plant, gave it a final sweep, decided he had done enough and went out through the window, to the fire escape. The fog was a relief after the hellish atmosphere inside, and Bolan made his way back down the ladder in a rush, unmindful of the noise, removing mask and goggles as he went. If they were waiting for him on the ground, against all odds, his Uzi was prepared to deal with any challenge that arose.

A handful of pedestrians had gathered on the sidewalk, staring at the club and speculating loudly on the sounds of battle that had issued from within. It stood to reason that police were on the way—or maybe not, considering the well-established code of silence that was second nature to the citizens of Chinatown. The vast majority of Asians in America were law-abiding folk, but many came to the United States with bloodred memories of how the laws had been enforced at home, and they were hesitant to deal with the authorities except when there was no alternative.

If anyone saw the tall man passing by in the fog, no sign was given, no alarm raised. Their focus was the building, intent on finding out what had befallen the proprietors and patrons.

Bolan left them to it, moving through the fog and back in the direction of his car. Round one of his attack on Sammy Ng was finished, and the Executioner was well ahead on points, but that could change at any moment.

He had to keep his guard up, all the way, or he could still be counted out, and losers never made a comeback in the kind of game that Bolan played.

His life was riding on the line, and he was backing it with everything he had.

2

Describing Sammy Ng as angry, when he heard the news about the club, would have been the understatement of the year. Within the space of ninety seconds, he had gone from calm to furious, with pit stops for amazement, disbelief and simple rage. It took that long for him to comprehend exactly what had happened, what the cleanup was about to cost him, and to grapple with the implications of a war about to break around his ears.

It was the first real challenge to his personal authority in Chinatown since Ng had taken office as the red pole of the ruling Triad three years earlier. Before that he had dealt with various opponents and competitors, both large and small, in sundry ruthless ways. His generosity and rage were legendary traits in Chinatown. Ng was the first to write a check when local charities had need of cash, the last man to forget an insult or an injury until the debt had been repaid—in blood.

He hadn't gained that reputation, or the red pole's rank, by hiding in the shadows, begging help from others. Ng took charge of problems and defeated them, the way a general in the army crushed hostile troops. Remorse and indecision were emotional conditions he refused to recognize.

But he was puzzled now, and worried.

The puzzlement was natural, all things considered. As the godfather of Chinatown, he was supposed to be immune to random violence, from his own or from the round-eyes who disgraced themselves at every opportunity. Between his troops, his reputation and his payoffs to assorted law-enforcement agencies, Ng should have had protection on a par with tenants of the White House. Still, for all that, some audacious bastards had seen fit to raid the Lung Cheung Club and trash his largest cutting plant.

It was unthinkable, but it had happened.

And that made Ng worry as he sat behind his massive antique desk, smoking and staring at the telephone. He didn't want to make the call, but there was no alternative. He couldn't hide the night's events from Luk Pang for any length of time; the man had eyes and ears all over Chinatown. There was a chance that he had heard the news already, but he wouldn't call to ask. Instead, he would judge Ng by the length of time it took him to resolve the problem or request assistance from outside.

No problem yet, as far as the red pole could see. He had been waiting for the last reports from Hangah Street to fill him in on monetary losses, body count, the neighborhood response to sudden mayhem in the night. Police hadn't been summoned—that would tell in Ng's favor, when the score was added up—and it would only take a day or so to get the club reopened, with the cutting plant restored to full production. On the down side, he had lost three million dollars' worth of China white, five soldiers and eleven drones from the production line. Among the peasant workers, only four were killed outright, but the survivors had inhaled sufficient heroin to hook an elephant. It would be cheaper to dispose of them than wait around and see which ones survived the next few hours, only to require expensive rehabilitation at a detox center.

Ng had passed that order on at once, and had had no second thoughts about the deaths of seven men and women who had served him like devoted slaves. Emotional attachments to the hired help were a luxury that he couldn't afford, and he had more important problems to contend with at the moment.

Like the question of his faceless enemy's identity, for starters.

The red pole had no idea, as yet, why anyone would take the risk of striking out at him this way. He had his share of enemies, and then some; it wasn't a question of his being loved by all who knew him. Rather, Ng was *feared,* and that meant more in Chinatown than any measure of respect.

None of the cutting plant survivors could describe the man or men who staged the raid. Ng knew his adversary was efficient and professional, but that put him no closer to a name. He would have felt more comfortable stalling Luk Pang until he had a better feel for what had happened, *why* it happened, but he also knew it could take days for all the answers to reveal themselves.

If ever.

Ng cut off that line of thought before it had a chance to undermine his confidence. He *would* root out his enemies and punish them for this insult. The Dragon *would* be pleased with his response, despite inevitable irritation that the incident had ever taken place.

All Ng had to do was scour San Francisco and environs for the man—or men—with guts enough to challenge him at home, in Chinatown, with no apparent motive for the act.

But first he had to make a call.

It was a local number. Luk Pang spent half his time in San Francisco, half in New York City. It was Ng's bad luck that he would be in town just when the shit went down.

Was that coincidence?

It made no sense to think that Pang would have had a hand in what happened at the club. They were together, bonded in a common cause, despite the outward differences of politics. There was a new day coming, when the mainland government regained control of Hong Kong and Macau. Adjustments would be necessary, but the top men in Beijing were wise enough to know that money talked. The mess in Russia had persuaded them of that, and they were changing as the need arose.

The very fact of the Red Dragon's existence was proof of that.

He tapped the number out from memory and listened while the other telephone rang once, twice, three times. Someone picked up then, but said nothing, waiting. Ng used his code name, just in case the line had sprouted extra ears, and waited through a silent interval for the familiar voice.

"How are you, Sammy?" Luk Pang inquired.

"Okay. Is this line clear?"

"Of course."

"I have a problem."

"At the Lung Cheung Club?"

"You heard." It came as no surprise.

"No details," Pang informed him, lying through his teeth. "I knew you'd call if there was any cause for worry."

"Well, I wouldn't go that far...."

"Have you identified the men responsible?"

"Not yet."

"That has to be the first priority," Pang said.

"I understand. We're working on it."

"If our friend should ask..."

"Just tell him I'm on top of it. No problem."

"I'm relieved to hear it."

"Probably a bunch of youngbloods, working on a reputation."

"Even so, it's bad for business," Pang replied.

"I can assure you, they won't get away with it."

"I hope not, Sammy. Bad publicity is one thing that we don't need at the moment."

"Understood. I'll keep you posted."

"If there's anything that I can do to help..."

"Not yet. I'll let you know."

"Don't hesitate to call."

"No. Thanks, I won't."

"I'll be here if you need me."

"Sure. Good night."

He cradled the receiver, furious to find that he was sweating. In his anger, Ng wished that he could reach through the phone line, grab Pang by the throat and choke him—long enough, at least, to wipe the smug expression off his face. He could see the bastard now, relaxing in his velvet smoking jacket, maybe picking up the telephone to call Macau.

But there was nothing he could do about Luk Pang. The only way to keep himself in favor with the Dragon was to do his job efficiently, and that meant tracking down the raiders of the club as soon as possible, inflicting punishment that would secure his reputation as the shadow boss of Chinatown.

He needed scalps for Pang, no later than the next day, even if he had to frame some street punks for the raid and take them out, to keep his own good name intact.

Whatever was required to save the situation, Sammy Ng would take it all the way. He hadn't come this far and worked this hard to see it all go up in smoke.

"YOU HAD GOOD FORTUNE."

It wasn't a question. Peter Fong looked somber as he faced the Executioner across a table in the corner of an all-night coffee shop on Stockton Street, a half mile north of Chinatown.

"It went all right," Bolan said.

"And my information was correct."

"It was."

Fong raised his teacup in a toast. "To victory. A new day for my people, when the Triad has been crushed."

"It may not be that simple," Bolan stated.

"I understand, of course. I am an optimist."

"That's fine, unless it makes you overconfident."

But overconfidence, the soldier realized, wasn't Fong's problem. As a businessman with solid roots in Chinatown, he knew exactly what could happen when civilians bucked the Triad's rule of iron. He could have named at least a dozen merchants like himself who had been terrorized with vandalism, arson, beatings and the like, when they initially refused to buy "protection" from the Chinese Mafia. At any given moment, Fong could have directed Immigration to a score of sweatshops where undocumented aliens were worked like slaves, producing inexpensive clothes and novelties, their weekly income barely adequate to pay the rent and keep their bellies full. He could have turned in prostitutes, drug dealers, maybe one or two professional assassins...but he had refrained from calling the police.

It was a cruel but simple twist of fate that prompted Peter Fong to break his silence, after years of paying tribute to the Triad and ignoring violence in his own backyard. A favorite nephew's death from heroin, a shot of China white some dealer on the street had cut with strychnine to reduce his operating costs, galvanized Fong into action. But even then the merchant didn't trust police in San Francisco to investigate the case. He didn't trust the FBI or DEA. Fong *did* have friends in Washington, however, dating from a previous Republican administration, and one of them made a call. The word got back to Hal Brognola, meshing with other news the big Fed was receiving out of the Far East, and so a switch was tripped at Stony Man.

Two days after Hal Brognola took that call, the Executioner was on his way to San Francisco, following the Dragon spoor.

"My confidence resides in you," Fong said.

The Executioner didn't waste time with self-effacing modesty. He knew what he could do, and Peter Fong had known what to expect when he reached out to Washington for help. The merchant cherished no illusions that he was participating in some kind of an elaborate sting that would result in Sammy Ng's arrest, indictment and conviction in a court of law. He wanted prompt and practical relief, for both himself and the people of Chinatown.

"I've got a foot in," Bolan told his contact, "but we've barely gotten started. Once he's sweating, then I'll take a run at Luk Pang."

Fong sipped his tea, making no reply. His tip about the Triads joining hands with Red Chinese illegals in the States had been the key to getting Stony Man involved in what would otherwise have been regarded as a local turf war, possibly a problem for the FBI or DEA to handle. In the past, the Triads had devoted some considerable energy—and cash—to sabotaging the Red rulers in Beijing. The Communists had done their best to drive the Tongs and Triads out of China back in 1949, and since crime families thrived on their own twisted version of free enterprise, the ultimate alliance of anti-Communist crusaders with organized crime had been a natural. Today, though, with nearly half a century elapsed since the People's Revolution in China, there was no end in sight to the Beijing regime. Hong Kong would revert to mainland control in 1997, and Macau two years later, leaving the people of "nationalist" Taiwan cut off and stranded from their homeland. Taiwanese leaders were already making conciliatory noises, while Red Chinese diplomats had been forging new ties with the West for more than a decade.

The fall of Russian communism and the resultant chaos in Moscow, including the rise of a brutally efficient "Russian Mafia," had taught the Chinese something in regard to preparation for the future. Based on rumbles from the vast Pacific Rim and Peter Fong's detailed reports from San Francisco, the alliance was already established, growing stronger by the day. The Beijing government, if so inclined, could help the Triads move more heroin than they had ever dreamed of, facilitate the flow of arms and other contraband, even tolerate business as usual in Hong Kong and

Macau—but such cooperation had a price. In return for Communist largess, the Triads would agree to lend a hand in the political arena—spying, punishing defectors, silencing dissent among Chinese in foreign countries, staging acts of sabotage, whatever. Bolan knew the possibilities were endless.

They were also terrifying.

He had come to San Francisco looking for a handle on the problem, hoping Peter Fong could help him find one, and he wasn't disappointed. In Sammy Ng, he faced one of the top three Triad leaders in America. With Luk Pang on hand and fronting for Beijing, it made a deadly combination, worthy of the Executioner's attention.

"Are you covered?" Bolan asked his contact.

"Covered?"

Bolan frowned. "Protected. Is your family safe?"

Fong answered with the bare suggestion of a shrug. "My only son is married, living in Los Angeles. My daughters are in college—one at Princeton, one at UC Santa Barbara. With any luck, the Triad will forget about them. Otherwise, who knows?"

"Your wife?"

"Deceased."

"I'm sorry."

"Such is life," Fong said. "I'm not afraid of death, per se, but I will not pretend I'm anxious to accelerate the process, either."

"If I play my cards right," Bolan said, "Ng shouldn't trace his problems back to you. But I'd be lying if I said there was no risk involved."

"We all face risks in Chinatown these days," Fong replied. "You've heard the stories, I suppose, about how smart and honest Asians are?"

"Word gets around."

"We're simply human, Mr. Blanski," Fong informed him, using Bolan's cover name. "If our approach to work or education seems a bit more strenuous than average, it is something we have learned from generations past. As for the other, China has been famous for her bandits from the earliest of times. We have our predators and victims, just like any other race—and sometimes we need help.''

''That's why I'm here.''

''As for your methods,'' Fong continued, ''leniency toward lawbreakers has never been a trademark of my people. In Beijing, today, the firing squads still execute drug dealers, rapists, even certain thieves. The Triads who have spread their cancer into foreign lands deserve no less.''

''The difference is, they won't be lined up with their backs against a wall. From what I've seen and heard, they don't lie down without a fight.''

''I take precautions,'' Fong assured him.

''Fair enough. Just so you're not surprised when they start hitting back.''

''I won't be.''

''Have you got the list?''

''Right here.''

An envelope changed hands. Inside would be a list of names and addresses, including Triad targets and assorted members of the ChiCom net. With any luck, it would be all that Bolan needed to complete the first phase of his mission. He didn't delude himself that it would end in San Francisco, though.

The Executioner was starting out along a hellfire trail, with no clear view of where that trail would take him. He would have to wait and see.

And to accomplish that, he had to stay alive.

IT WAS A CHALLENGE for a man like Luk Pang to live and work in the United States. At forty-one, he had been raised from birth to view America as The Enemy, alternately scorned as a paper tiger and reviled for its insidious conspiracies around the globe. He saw no contradiction in the two opposing views, since Chairman Mao was said to be politically infallible. It didn't matter that the view on Western life had changed somewhat in recent years. Luk Pang still recognized his enemy and understood his duty to the People's Revolution.

For any dedicated Communist, residing in America was both a challenge and a strange adventure. There were pitfalls in American society, apparent contradictions that conflicted with the atheistic gospel Pang had learned at home. Racism and division of the classes *did* exist, for instance, but America wasn't the giant concentration camp that Mao and his disciples had described. In fact, the poorest ghetto residents in San Francisco and New York had more, in terms of worldly goods, than the majority of Chinese citizens. There seemed to be no lynchings anymore, though racial violence cut both ways. Police were sometimes brutal, but the worst offenders went to prison, just like common criminals. In Washington, the President and Congress spent more time debating prayer in schools and budgetary matters than the secret war on socialism.

All of that could be explained, of course. A true believer always read between the lines, held fast to the conviction that the enemies he couldn't see were those who posed the greatest threat. Pang understood how easy it would be to let the decadent society seduce him, fill his mind with nonsense and distract him from his duty, but he had a warrior's dedication to the cause. Prepared to sacrifice his life, if necessary, Pang still cared enough about survival to prepare for swift evacuation in a pinch—and to assure himself that in the last extremity, he wouldn't die alone.

It had disgusted him, at first, to work in concert with the Triads, long reviled as filthy running dogs of the oppressor. Now that leaders of the largest criminal fraternity had struck a bargain with Beijing, however, Pang raised no objection when he was assigned to guide them through their paces. To a diehard revolutionary, every ounce of heroin that entered the United States was one more bullet fired into the body of his adversary; each illegal immigrant who found a hiding place in San Francisco, New York or Los Angeles was a potential agent of the People's Revolution, waiting for his orders to arrive. The network was expanding daily, while the round-eyed idiots in Washington poured money into China, signed new trade agreements and retreated from their stand on so-called "human rights" like the pathetic, spineless dogs they were.

Pang had actually come to relish his position in the States. The operation gave him an unprecedented opportunity to live the part of a devoted mercenary capitalist, even as he worked to undermine the money-grubbing system. Never mind that Beijing's current rulers had incorporated many of the Western traits and mores into daily Chinese life—from clothing styles and television programs to McDonald's restaurants—while still asserting dedication to the rule of communism. Pang had faith that any move his masters made could only serve the cause, just as he did, pushing on toward final victory.

When that day came, the Triads would be swept aside with all the other human garbage, rounded up and executed for their crimes against the people. In the meantime, though, it wouldn't hurt to use them as unwitting tools, cash in on their prodigious greed and turn their energy toward the destruction of the very system that perpetuated their existence.

Pang wasn't a poet, but he had a feeling for poetic justice, all the same. It made him smile to think of how the drug lords and their followers would wail and gnash their teeth when it was time to pay their debts.

Meanwhile, ironically, Pang was assigned to keep them fat and healthy, while the silent war went on. And that meant helping Sammy Ng resolve his latest problem in the heart of Chinatown.

Ng's trouble was a minor inconvenience, so far, but it could get out of hand if they didn't respond effectively. Pang knew enough of criminals to understand their thinking, how a leader who showed evidence of weakness would be swept aside by stronger men. And while he had no personal regard for Ng, it would be inconvenient, after all this time, if he was forced to start from the beginning and negotiate a brand-new bargain with some other thug.

A setback of that nature would infuriate the Dragon, throwing off his whole timetable. There would be painful repercussions up and down the line, with Pang on tap for the most drastic punishment.

Reluctantly he made up his mind to assist the red pole with his problem, as much as possible. Pang had no intention of exposing himself to personal danger for something so trivial, but he could mobilize his resources if necessary, should Ng's private army prove inadequate in dealing with the situation. It was critical, he realized, to keep their solid front intact for the time being, while the Triads were still useful to Beijing.

Step one in solving the red pole's problem would be learning the identity of those responsible for his discomfort. Pang had many eyes and ears in Chinatown, some of them still unknown to Ng. It would be most unusual, he thought, for an event like the attack on the Lung Cheung Club to pass without some comment—boasting, for example, or complaints—from those responsible. Thugs liked to talk about their crimes, impressing women and one another, building up their reputations on the street. If someone dared to challenge Sammy Ng in Chinatown, it stood to reason that the upstart's name would soon be known.

Unless...

Pang caught himself before the thought took shape, sat back and frowned. Suppose the enemy wasn't from Chinatown? What then?

A round-eye?

When Ng first came to San Francisco, there had been a problem with the Mafia, but after some initial bloodshed, Ng had signed a truce with the Italians, and the problem went away...or had it?

Pang considered the potential repercussions of an inter-racial gang war breaking out just now, when they were on the verge of kicking off the Dragon's master plan. He scowled, deciding someone should reach out to the Italians, try to learn if they had staged the raid on the club. If they were innocent, perhaps their sources could be tapped for further information, as the need arose.

In any case, the problem had to be resolved, and soon. There would be no forgiveness if the Dragon's plans were put on hold, no smiling acquiescence. If anything derailed the operation, heads would surely roll, and Pang wasn't prepared to sacrifice himself for someone else's clumsy error.

He would give the red pole time, but not too much. If things weren't resolved within twenty-four hours, Pang would have to do the job himself.

3

The Walther WA-2000 was a first rate sniper rifle, custom tailored for the kind of urban killing zone where Bolan found himself. Barely three feet long, the weapon was a bull pup model, with its magazine behind the pistol grip and trigger, thus reducing length and helping out with balance. The free-floating barrel was anchored fore and aft, fluted to assist in cooling and reduce vibrations. With its ten-power telescopic sight and a full load of .300 Winchester Magnum rounds, the Walther scored consistent kills at better than a thousand yards.

This night, though, Bolan would be shooting from about one-tenth that distance. Complicating factors were geography, the presence of civilian bystanders and the distinct possibility that his targets would be shooting back.

The first two problems were beyond his control. You had to take the targets where you found them—which, in this case, meant a rooftop stakeout on the Chinese Recreation Center, at Washington and Mason. Bolan's car was parked below, and a toolbox beside him would hold the rifle once he broke it down. He would have to deal with any close-range opposition as it came.

Pedestrians were unavoidable in Chinatown, regardless of the hour. They shouldn't be a problem, Bolan thought, unless his adversaries opened fire at random on the street. The quickest way to nip that problem in the bud would be to take out his targets swiftly and efficiently, before they had a chance to fight or run away.

The faces of the three men were burned into his mind, subjects of Polaroid pictures that Peter Fong had given him. His targets weren't criminals, in the accepted sense, though each would have faced prison time if their activities in Chinatown had been revealed. They were illegals—covert agents of the Beijing government—involved in spying and assorted other acts that "friendly" nations were expected to avoid. One of them had recruited three enlisted men at the Presidio to feed him information on troop movements and the like. Another had his finger on the pulse of labor unions in the San Francisco area. The third divided up his time between the University of California Berkeley campus, where he had admirers in the college crowd, and Oakland's ghetto, where he was well-known among black "militants" of the felonious variety. It was suspected that he was responsible for Chinese automatic weapons reaching local street gangs, but there was no evidence that would have passed the necessary courtroom tests.

Which was fine.

Bolan wasn't bound by rules of evidence. He had no jury to convince, no fat elected boss to satisfy with a "politically correct" solution to the problem. As a soldier, he was trained to find the most efficient route to reach his goal.

Downrange, he saw the front door of the recreation center open, and three men stepped onto the sidewalk. One of them directed a teenaged valet to fetch their car.

He checked each face through the scope, confirming the ID, then scanned around them briefly, making sure that bullet fragments and ricochets wouldn't endanger passersby. Peering down from rooftop level, Bolan had no problem with the fog. The valet was returning with a shiny Lincoln Town Car as the scope picked out a face and framed it, cross hairs frozen at a point above the moving lips.

He took a deep breath, held it, as his index finger tightened on the Walther's trigger, taking up the slack. All he had to do was sight and squeeze.

The rifle bucked against his shoulder, Bolan holding steady on the mark. His target blurred for just a heartbeat, the motion of the rifle merging with a splash of crimson as the hollowpoint projectile found its mark, then he was tracking to his left, already settled on another face before its owner could react.

A woman's scream reached Bolan as he fired the second shot, the Walther's silencer effective only to a point. It could suppress the sound of firing, but a supersonic round produced its own noise once it left the muzzle, like a tiny jet in flight. No silencer on earth could deal with that sound, but he counted on distraction, speed and echoes from surrounding storefronts to confuse potential witnesses.

The second man was gaping at his fallen comrade when a bullet struck him just below one eye and punched him over on his back. By that time, number three was bolting for the recreation center's open door, aware of mortal danger, even if he didn't recognize the source. It was no more than ten or fifteen feet, an easy run, but in the present circumstance it might as well have been a mile.

The guy was halfway through his second stride when Bolan stroked the Walther's trigger one more time and slammed a hollowpoint between his shoulder blades. Momentum and the force of impact helped him reach the building, but his aim was off, and Bolan watched him slam facefirst into the wall. Rebounding like a crash test dummy, he collapsed onto the sidewalk in a spreading pool of crimson.

Fifteen seconds later Bolan had the rifle broken down and stowed inside his toolbox, and he was moving toward the service stairs. There was no one to challenge him or note a round-eye passing in the night before he reached his car. If anyone remembered him, the witness would recall a faded jumpsuit with the logo of a nonexistent air-conditioning repair firm printed on the back, a baseball cap pulled low to hide his face. A quick glance at the rearview mirror revealed that no one was studying the rental's license plate as he pulled out and drove away.

All clear.

He didn't have to check the printed list from Peter Fong to know where he was going next. The targets were imprinted in his mind, the next one rolling up to assume its place as Bolan scratched its predecessor from the list.

TOMMY LING HAD BEEN assigned to guard the house on Duncombe Street. It wasn't like a *real* house, where real people lived—although, when Tommy stopped to think about it, he supposed the girls had to spend the best part of their time there. Female service for a male was still a part of old Chinese tradition, and the girls who staffed the house on Duncombe Street were mostly just off the boat, illegals working off their debts—or so they thought. Between the shame, the drugs and the lousy pay, few of them would ever "graduate" to hit the streets and look for honest work, much less go on to have a family. When they began to lose their looks, those who were functional at anything but lying on their backs could make the trade-off to a sweatshop, while a brand-new crop of Asian beauties took their place between the sheets.

They could expect no sympathy from Tommy Ling. He was supposed to keep them safe, which meant he handled rowdy johns and was prepared to deal with anybody who came rolling in specifically to cause a scene, but he was also there to keep the girls in line, make sure none of them slipped away or gave the old housemother any lip. He was a combination bodyguard and jailer, working overtime to be a wealthy, famous gangster.

Just like Sammy Ng.

Their names were even similar, which Ling took for an omen of good fortune. You could never really tell, of course, but he was hopeful. If he watched his step and didn't blow his money like an idiot, he would be halfway there. The other half would take some luck and ingenuity, however. He would have to pray for something that would bring him to the red pole's personal attention—in a beneficial way, of course; no screw-ups, thank you very much—and lead Ng to consider all the benefits that would accrue to him and to the family from moving Tommy up in rank.

In fact, he thought, the trouble at the Lung Cheung Club might just turn out to be a blessing in disguise.

No one had challenged Ng in Chinatown for several years now. That was good for business, but it limited a soldier's opportunities for showing off to the boss. There were occasions when the word came down for Tommy Ling to break some welsher's legs, or torch a shop whose owner had decided it was safe to live without protection from the family, but that was grunt work, something every member of the Triad took for granted. What he needed now was either something in the nature of a plum assignment—damned unlikely, he admitted to himself—or else a major stroke of luck.

A war increased his odds of getting lucky, just as it increased his odds of getting dead. Ling smiled, imagining a scene with Ng alighting from his limo, Ling standing by, when someone on a rooftop opened fire. In his imagination, he leaped in front of Ng and took the bullet, and the grateful boss rewarded him in regal style.

Keep dreaming, Ling told himself, and checked his watch. Five minutes past the hour, and he still had four to go before his day relief showed up, assuming that the lazy bum would even be on time.

The whorehouse watch wasn't exactly Ling's notion of a good job, even with a war—or maybe just a skirmish—coming down. He would be sidelined, damn it, while his young, ambitious brothers grabbed the glory for themselves. Ling wondered if there was a way for him to swing a transfer, get out on the street while there was still some hope of action. Given what he heard about the Lung Cheung raid, it stood to reason Sammy would be searching high and low for those responsible, which meant that they would soon be found and brought to book—at least if they were residents of Chinatown. If it was someone else, though, Ling knew the hunt could take a while. There might be other raids before the enemy could be identified and run to ground.

He switched on the big-screen television and was channel-surfing in a search of something that would catch his fancy, when the old housemother started calling out to him. She didn't sound excited or upset—a little strained, perhaps, but that was just her way. Ling turned off the TV and went to find out what her problem was. A leaky faucet, maybe, or a peanut butter shortage in the kitchen. Ling wasn't a handyman or gofer, and the old woman knew it, but he had to make the point with her repeatedly, week after week, as if she thought it were some kind of stupid game.

Emerging from the TV room, Ling stopped dead in his tracks and blinked, trying to make sense of what he saw. A tall white man was standing with the old housemother, one hand on her shoulder, while the other held an Uzi trained on Ling's chest.

"You're it?"

Ling wasn't sure how he should answer that. It sounded something like an insult, but the submachine gun made it difficult for him to take offense. Instead of answering, he came back with a question of his own.

"What's going on?"

"You're closing for repairs. There's a fire."

Ling listened for a smoke alarm, sniffed at the air and said, "I don't smell anything."

"It hasn't started yet."

"This is a big mistake," he said, trying to be cocky without forcing the intruder to shoot. You didn't need a brain the size of all outdoors to draw a link between this shooter and the Lung Cheung Club.

"Your choice boils down to live or die." The white man didn't sound pissed off or menacing, more like a life insurance salesman laying out the options on a policy.

And something spoke to Tommy Ling, told him that he would never have a better chance to prove himself. If he could drop the round-eye where he stood, it would protect the house *and* put his boss one long step closer to avenging the attack against the club. All Ling had to do was reach inside his jacket, pull the Browning double-action automatic from its pancake holster and blow the guy away. If something happened to the old housemother in the process, what the hell? Old women were replaceable, the same as young ones.

All he needed was the nerve.

"Time's up," the white man told him, and before he knew it, Ling was dropping to a crouch, his right hand going for the pistol, while his left made little twitching motions out of sympathy.

He never cleared the holster, barely had his fingers wrapped around the pistol's butt when flame exploded from the Uzi's muzzle and he felt the bullets ripping through his shoulder, rib cage, abdomen. The world slid out from under him, and Ling went down on his backside, kept on going until his skull bounced on the floor.

It didn't really hurt that much. There was a creeping warmth, then numbness. It was hard to focus on the white man bending over him, inspecting him with eyes that didn't give a damn.

"Start rounding up the girls," the intruder told the lady of the house. "You haven't got much time."

And neither did Tommy Ling.

THE SUITE OF ROOMS that Sammy Ng called home took up three-quarters of the top floor of a small but elegant hotel on Waverly, several blocks from the Lung Cheung Club. The remaining top-floor rooms were occupied by soldiers whose sole duty was to keep the red pole safe from harm. It stood to reason they would all be packing, with some medium to heavy weapons in reserve. If Bolan meant to pull it off, surprise and sheer audacity would be his greatest allies.

Bolan parked his vehicle three doors down from the hotel, not bothering to lock it. Car theft wasn't a major risk in Chinatown, unlike the rest of San Francisco, and the thanks for that, ironically, was owed in large part to the Triad, for discouraging the kind of petty street crime that was rampant nationwide.

It was still foggy as he left the car and moved along the sidewalk, ducking down a narrow alley south of the hotel. He found the service entrance and attacked the lock with slender metal picks. In less than sixty seconds he was standing in a corridor that served the hotel's kitchen, laundry room and storage area.

The service elevator would have been an easy ride, but it would also telegraph his ascent to the penthouse guards. He took the stairs instead, unlimbering the Uzi as he climbed and wondering if it was all for nothing. Ng could well be at his office, maybe even on the street by now, a general rallying his troops.

No matter.

If he missed the boss of Chinatown this time, at least he would have sent a message back to Ng that there was nowhere he could hide. In either case, the loss of personnel would shave the odds a little more, disrupt morale for the survivors.

Twelve flights of stairs took Bolan to the sixth floor of the small hotel, and he met no opposition on the way. A warning had been painted on his side of the metal door: This Door to Remain Unlocked by Order of the Fire Marshal.

Bolan offered a silent thanks to his unwitting ally on the fire department, edging close to peer through a smallish window with wire mesh set into the glass.

As far as he could see, the corridor beyond that door was empty, but his view was limited to left and right. There could be ten or twenty gunners in the hall, for all he knew, but Bolan doubted it. The standard live-in complement was six, according to the information passed along by Peter Fong. It would be a coin toss as to whether the soldier's recent raids increased that number or subtracted from it, sending barracks gunners out to prowl the streets.

In any case, he had no option. He would have to cross that threshold if he meant to deal with Sammy Ng, and every moment he delayed was wasted time.

His left hand found the metal pressure bar, and Bolan grimaced as the door squeaked slightly, opening. He shouldered through behind the Uzi, checking to his right because he was exposed on that side first, but there was no challenge from the empty corridor.

The door hissed shut behind him, and he pivoted to check the hallway on his left. A lone young man stood facing him, uncertain what to make of this intrusion by a white until he saw the deadly subgun. The smart thing, even then, would have been for the guy to throw up his hands in surrender, but his pride and sense of duty forced a very different response.

The gunner had no weapon showing, but he did his best to remedy that situation, popping buttons on his jacket as he ripped it open, reaching for the pistol holstered underneath his arm. He had only fractions of a second left to live and might have known it, since he cried out for his backup before he made his move.

The Uzi stuttered through its silencer and four 9 mm rounds stitched drooling holes across the young man's chest. The impact staggered him and froze his hand a critical six inches short of hardware as he toppled over, lifeless, on his back.

Beyond the sprawling corpse, two doors swung open almost simultaneously, one on each side of the corridor. Two gunners barged out on his left, both holding pistols, while a third young man, in boxer shorts, emerged on Bolan's right, a riot shotgun in his hands.

It took a moment for the three hardmen to scope out what was happening, and that was all the time they had. Their enemy was braced for action, tracking with the Uzi, holding down its trigger as he swept the corridor from left to right and back again. The Triad gunners twitched and capered through a jerky dance of death as bullets found them, spun them on their heels and dropped them squirming on the floor.

Before another target surfaced, the Executioner moved back along the hallway, toward the door that opened into Ng's hideaway.

A short burst from the Uzi blew the doorknob off and dropped it on the floor. He followed with a flying kick and charged across the threshold, ducking as a storm of bullets rattled overhead.

THE GODFATHER of Chinatown was watching the reigning porn queen on video and waiting for the next round of reports from troopers on the street, when someone shouted in the hall outside his suite. He didn't recognize the voice, but Ng was instantly alert, aware that only mortal danger could have prompted such a cry.

He killed the video and scrambled for his automatic in the nightstand drawer. Out front, two gunners in the living room were moving toward the door to find out what was happening, but Ng saw them hesitate as something grim and terrible transpired outside.

His men were dying out there. Ng could tell it, even though the raider's gun was obviously fitted with a silencer. The sound of bodies falling, doors thrown open, bullets smacking into plaster—all were unmistakable to anyone who fought his way up from the streets to rule a Triad family by force and fear. The fact that none of Ng's men were shooting back told him their fate, as certainly as if he had been standing there and watching them go down.

"Get ready!" Ng shouted to the gunmen in his living room. One of them muttered an acknowledgment, then they separated to flank the entryway, still visibly reluctant to expose themselves by opening the door.

That part of it was fine with Ng. He didn't want his enemies *inside* the suite, for God's sake, not if there was still a chance to keep them out. He reached out for the telephone, uncertain whether he should punch up 911 or call one of his field lieutenants back to help.

Before the choice was made, he heard a ripping sound and watched in horror as a burst of automatic fire tore through his front door, shattering the lock on impact. Ng's men were still recoiling from the blast when someone gave the door a solid kick and came through in a rush. Ng had a fleeting image of a tall man, armed, before he sprang across the room and slammed his bedroom door.

His men were firing wildly in the other room, the gunshots cracking out in rapid fire. From where he crouched, behind the bed, Ng heard the muffled stutter of his adversary's weapon—only one piece from the sound of it—and then, once more, the unmistakable sound of bodies hitting the floor.

He bolted for the door to the adjacent bathroom, and almost made it through before another burst of automatic fire stitched holes across his bedroom door and punched it inward, swinging wide. Ng slammed the bathroom door behind him, pressed the button on its flimsy lock and backed into the sunken simulated-marble tub. In there, with any luck, he might at least be safe from ricochets.

He heard the stalker cross his bedroom, moving cautiously. Ng aimed his pistol at the door and waited, angry at his hands for trembling as they gripped the weapon.

Ng believed that he was ready to defend himself, but he recoiled with a pathetic cry of fear as bullets started chewing up the bathroom door. Its lock exploded, and the shattered knob came wobbling toward him, like some broken toy that stubbornly refused to die. The door swung open, inch by inch, and Ng found the nerve to trigger three quick rounds, aware before he pulled the trigger that they would be wasted.

At first he didn't recognize the metal egg-shaped object that came flying through the doorway on the heels of his wild shots. It took a heartbeat for his mind to come up with the word *grenade,* and then he bolted, panic taking over, certain that he would be torn apart in seconds by the blast and rending shrapnel.

He was well across the bathroom threshold when he recognized his critical mistake. By that time, automatic fire was ripping through his legs like white-hot daggers, bringing him down. He lost his pistol, gasping, breathless in his agony, and only hoped that death would follow swiftly. Maybe, when the hand grenade went off...

But it didn't explode.

Instead, he felt a rough hand on his shoulder and grimaced with the pain as someone rolled him over on his back. From Ng's perspective, the white man was upside down. He would have laughed in other circumstances, but the pain precluded that.

"I didn't pull the pin," his adversary said. "You're not much good at poker, are you?"

Ng swallowed his embarrassment with blood, from where his teeth had gouged the inside of his cheek, and tried to find his voice.

"Who are you?"

"Your judgment."

"What?"

"Just listen up. You don't have lots of time, and I need answers."

"Answers."

"Luk Pang," the stranger said. "Where can I find him."

Ng thought about it for a moment, wondering how far his honor would require him to extend himself before he died. There seemed to be no question of survival in the present circumstances, since his adversary didn't even deign to hide his face. No threat of retribution from the Triad mattered to a corpse. Still . . .

"This came down on you because of Pang," the gunman said. "Your dealings with Beijing. What do you owe him, anyway?"

"I don't know."

"You don't know *what*?"

"Where you can find him now."

"Wrong answer."

Ng saw the submachine gun's muzzle moving closer to his face. Nine millimeter, almost certainly, and yet it looked so large. While he was focused on the gun, a foot prodded one of his wounded legs.

He screamed the address without thinking, as if any words could save him now. Perhaps, if nothing else, the sacrifice of Pang would spare him further suffering.

His tormentor moved toward the bathroom, dawdled for a moment, then came back. He stooped beside the fallen godfather of Chinatown, tucking something round and warm beneath his arm.

"I'll keep the pin this time," he said, already moving toward the door and out of range. He was outside the suite and jogging toward the stairs when an explosion smothered Ng's hopeless scream.

4

Luk Pang had found himself a place to live outside of Chinatown, if only by a block or two. His town house, situated in the middle of the block on Fallon, was a short walk south from Coolbrith Park, just north of Broadway and Chinatown proper. Bolan, navigating through the fog, had time to wonder if his adversary chose the house deliberately, to set himself apart from those among his countrymen he sought to use, or if the choice was mere coincidence.

No matter.

Bolan had a fix on Pang, and he was going through the jugular. With Sammy Ng eliminated, it would take some time for members of the Triad to select another red pole to replace him. There was certain to be disagreement in the ranks, and Hong Kong headquarters would have to be involved. Meanwhile, the time had come for him to strike at the Asian Hydra's political head, while the mercenary criminal side thrashed about and licked its wounds.

He had already started on the Reds, with his attack outside the Chinese Recreation Center, but long experience had taught him that all revolutionaries were expendable. While thinning the ranks would have some value, when it came to scuttling certain operations, breaking down morale, the surest way to bring down a cadre was to attack the leadership and keep on the pressure until the grass-roots body of the movement lost direction, started to disintegrate. You couldn't help but give the Reds some martyrs in the process, but a legend needed time to grow, some tender loving care along the way, and men didn't care much for saints or martyrs while you kept them running for their lives.

He made a drive-by, checked out the town house and marked the gunmen lounging in a car out front. It would be no great challenge to dispose of them, but Bolan had to guess that sentries posted on the street meant lookouts in the house, as well. He would be spotted, either coming up the street or taking out the first two guards, and that would sacrifice whatever edge surprise allowed him in the present situation.

He left the rental car near Coolbrith Park and walked back through the drifting fog to have a look around. The street was not on one of San Francisco's famous hills, which meant that he could pass from one roof to the next with no great difficulty, maybe find his way in through a service door or attic, if he could get up there in the first place.

The houses didn't come equipped with fire escapes or ladders mounted on the walls, but Bolan had been trained to improvise. They all had drain pipes, for example, fastened to the brick with heavy metal cleats. It wasn't all that far to climb for him to reach the roof. No more than thirty feet.

He reached into a pocket of his rain coat, found the leather driving gloves and slipped them on. His black athletic shoes would grip the pipe and brick as well as anything except bare feet, and he wasn't prepared to leave his shoes behind.

The climb was relatively simple, complicated mainly by the fact of his exposure to pedestrians and passing motorists. The fog and Bolan's timing helped in that regard, minimizing both traffic and visibility. If there was anyone awake on Fallon Street at that hour, aside from Luk Pang's bodyguards, they kept themselves well out of sight and brooded in the dark.

His feet slipped two or three times, and the drain pipe groaned once as Bolan reached the roof and scrambled clear, but it wasn't enough to rouse the sleeping tenants of the house. He paused a moment on the roof to stretch his muscles and survey the territory, spotting air conditioners and television aerials, his pencil flashlight picking out the service hatch that Bolan guessed would open on some kind of attic or crawlspace, or perhaps directly on some room upstairs. There was no topside latch or lock, which would have trapped the residents inside and made the hatchway useless. Figure on some kind of inner bolt or padlock, then, and he would have to take his chances breaking through.

He would concern himself with details when he got there, putting his trust in speed and firepower if stealth wasn't enough to do the job.

At least this way he had a fighting chance of taking Luk Pang by surprise. The other route, a straight charge from the street past waiting guns, was almost guaranteed to fail.

The Executioner moved on with cautious steps, and quickly vanished in the creeping fog.

LUK PANG LAY on his bed in darkness, wide awake and wondering why there had been no further word from Sammy Ng. The logical response to that would be that Ng had nothing to report. A mere three hours had elapsed since the invasion of the Lung Cheung Club, and it would be no simple task to ferret out suspects in Chinatown by night. Ng had his sources, granted, but there were no miracles in life, and everything took time.

Unfortunately Ng's problem was no longer limited to members of the Triad. Ninety minutes earlier, three close associates of Luk Pang had been gunned down outside the Chinese Recreation Center, evidently slain with long-range rifle fire by someone who possessed extraordinary skill. It was impossible for Pang to believe the two attacks, so closely linked in time and place, were unrelated.

If one man, or a group of men, had staged both incidents, it had to mean that Pang's connection to the Triad was exposed. How could that be? They had been cautious; Pang himself had seen to that, impressing the need for extra care on Sammy Ng and his superiors. It was impossible, of course, to guarantee that there would be no leaks or breakdowns in security, where human beings were involved.

Pang had to think in terms of damage now, while there was time, before a link between the two attacks was positively demonstrated. Part of his assignment in America, beyond cooperation with the Triads, was to keep his masters well advised of any problems, warn them of potential danger so that they could take the necessary steps.

The time had come, in his opinion, for a phone call Pang had hoped that he would never have to make.

He sat up, found the lamp by feel and switched it on. The sudden brightness made him blink as he was reaching for the telephone.

There was a special number in Macau that he had memorized for such emergencies. It would be manned around the clock, and while he wouldn't be allowed to speak directly with the man who pulled his strings, the message would be swiftly passed along. Pang would be forced to wait for a reply, but it shouldn't take long. A few more hours, give or take, meant nothing in the global scheme of things.

The telephone was dead.

There was no dial tone when he raised the handset to his ear. Pang tapped the plunger several times, but the line was well and truly dead.

He cradled the receiver, frowning. What did it mean? Pang checked the wall jack, knowing as he did so that the odds against an accidental disconnection were extreme. It was unlikely, also, that the telephone had simply ceased to function on its own. There was no storm outside, which would account for breakdowns in the system.

If he, and he alone, was cut off from the world outside, it had to mean trouble.

A sudden panic gripped him, made him tremble as he rose and reached out for his robe, draped carefully across a nearby chair. He pictured black-clad gunmen creeping through the house, his guards already slain downstairs.

Pang slipped into the robe and continued to his closet, where he knelt and drew a section of the carpet back. Secure from prying eyes, in case the house was ever searched, he kept a mini-Uzi submachine gun, loaded, with a few spare magazines.

Pang felt a bit ridiculous as he picked up the weapon, thumbed off its safety and slipped an extra magazine into the left-hand pocket of his robe, but it was better safe than sorry. If he was wrong, and the malfunction of the telephone was easily explained, he would channel his embarrassment into a stinging reprimand. But Pang didn't hire idiots to guard his home, and instinct told him there had been no clumsy accident, no drunken driver crashing into the phone poles down the block.

His enemies were on the way, perhaps already here.

Pang thought of taking time to dress, but it was more important, at the moment, to find out exactly what was happening. He had to know if they were already surrounded, if the outer guards had been eliminated while his other watchmen somehow overlooked the fact.

He had to know the worst, before the whole damned situation spun out of control.

Pang left his spacious bedroom, moving quickly toward the stairs. He held the mini-Uzi pressed against his leg, concealed, but kept his finger curled around the trigger.

Just in case.

THE ROOFS BOLAN CROSSED were basically identical, though he found the access hatch in a slightly different location on each one. He counted off six houses, stopping at the seventh, with his targets now directly underneath him.

Bolan clipped the telephone line with his knife as a precaution, then knelt beside the hatch and tried it with his fingers, just in case someone was negligent enough to leave the entryway unbolted. When it wouldn't budge, he spent another moment checking out the hinges, calculating where the lock or bolt had to be. He couldn't trust his knife to pry it open, and he didn't have a crowbar with him. He would have to blast it free and damn the consequences, put his faith in speed and accuracy once he got inside. A fair amount of noise was unavoidable, no matter how he tried to force the hatch, and bullets had the virtue of being a relatively swift solution to his problem.

Bolan rose, stepped back a pace and switched his Uzi onto single-shot mode. He aimed, squeezed off three rounds and saw the woodwork splinter, heard at least one of his bullets striking metal underneath.

This time when Bolan tried the hatch, it opened at his touch. Pitch darkness was underneath him, and he hesitated for a precious moment, listening for telltale sounds of a reaction from his enemies. He tried the penlight next and saw that he had been correct: the hatch gave access to a smallish attic, almost claustrophobic in dimension. Six or seven feet below, the remnants of a shattered hasp and padlock lay atop a stack of dusty cardboard boxes. Bolan's parabellum rounds had torn the box on top, but seemingly hadn't passed through to drill the attic floor.

He slung the Uzi, gripped the penlight in his teeth and cautiously descended, clinging with his hands to touch down softly in the attic, no unnecessary sounds of impact as he landed on tiptoes. The dust that covered everything was proof that Pang and company had seldom used the attic, if they even knew of its existence.

He found the exit hatch and crouched beside it, listening. If gunmen were waiting on the other side, they made no sound.

He raised the trapdoor with his left hand, leveling the Uzi in his right, the fire-selector switch thumbed back to automatic mode. The hinges didn't squeal, and Bolan blinked at darkness for another moment, listening again before he tried the pencil flash. Its light revealed a wooden shelf and a rack of hanging clothes below.

The trapdoor opened on a closet.

Bolan scrambled through and landed on his feet, the hanging clothes behind him rustling on their hangers. He was reaching for the inner doorknob when somebody started knocking on the bedroom door. A light came on, spilling underneath the closet door. A moment later he was listening to two male voices, an exchange in heated Mandarin. He couldn't translate, but the agitation of both speakers was apparent. One retreated, slamming the bedroom door behind him, and the other kept on muttering, making noises like somebody dressing in a rush.

Some kind of rumble. Were they bailing out?

His left hand found the doorknob, turned it and gave the closet door a shove. Eyes narrowed into slits against the light, he stepped into the bedroom proper and found a young Chinese there, gaping at him, with his shirt half-buttoned and his fly unzipped.

The gunman had good ears, though. He had given up on dressing to retrieve a pistol from the nightstand, and he had it aimed at Bolan's face.

FOUR SOLDIERS in the house and two outside. It wasn't much, in terms of personal defense, but Pang didn't maintain an army in the heart of San Francisco. He relied primarily on loaners from the Triad, plus a handpicked team of trusted aides. One of the latter, Hong Kong native Philip Soo, was seated at the breakfast counter, sipping coffee from a plastic mug, when Pang came downstairs in his robe, the mini-Uzi in his hand.

"Is something wrong, Luk?"

"Try the telephone. It's dead upstairs."

Soo left his stool and walked to the telephone mounted on the wall beside the built-in microwave. He lifted the receiver, listened for a moment, frowned and hung it up.

"Here, too."

A pair of Triad gunners joined them, coming from the living room. They didn't seem concerned, despite the recent violence in the city, but you couldn't always tell with mercenary types.

"What's wrong?" one of them asked.

"The telephones are dead," Pang told him. "Check the guards outside."

The gunner hurried to a window, drew the curtains back a foot or so and peered into the night. "Still there," he said.

"Are they *alive?*"

The young man blinked at Pang. "They're sitting up."

"Go out and check on them." Pang turned to his companion. "You, go up and wake the others. Tell them we are leaving."

Soo was always armed. It was a standing joke between them that he showered with a knife clenched in his teeth and never went to bed without a gun beneath his pillow. By the time Pang finished snapping orders at the two young gunmen, Soo had drawn a pistol from concealment on his person and had placed it on the breakfast bar, between them, with the muzzle pointed toward neutral ground.

"It may be nothing, Luk," he said.

"We can't take chances, Philip."

"No."

The gunman he had sent out to the street returned a moment later and closed the door behind him, shutting out the night.

"They're fine out there," he said. "They haven't seen a thing."

Pang frowned. He could be getting paranoid, but it was safer to bail out and find a new place to hide than to remain in place without communications, cut off from his allies, possibly surrounded by the enemy.

"We're leaving anyway," he said. "I'll go get dressed." He glanced at Soo. "You get the car."

Both men were moving off in opposite directions, Pang toward the stairs, his aide toward outer darkness, when a pistol shot rang out upstairs. The man at Pang's side produced a sawed-off shotgun out of nowhere. It was like some kind of magic trick.

"Stay here," the soldier said, and started toward the stairs.

No, thanks, Pang thought, and turned to follow Soo outside. He could replace the clothing left upstairs. Now, he simply wanted to get out of there alive.

IT WAS A TOSS-UP, which of them would pull the trigger first, and Bolan never really knew who won the call in terms of speed. His aim was better, though, assisted by the edge full-auto fire could give a well-trained shooter. Bolan heard the Chinese gunman's bullet smack the wall above his head, the echo of the shot loud in his ears, before the young man toppled over backward in a lifeless sprawl.

Kiss the surprise goodbye.

He couldn't even count on Luk Pang's soldiers being groggy, half-asleep, since one of them, at least, had left this very room brief moments earlier. That made at least three gunners up and at it, with the troops outside, and from the hasty conversation he had overheard, it sounded as if the house was being roused to action.

He reached the bedroom door in four long strides and threw it open, poked his head out for a glance along the corridor, then put the room behind him. To his left, the stairs lay open and unguarded at the moment. On his right, another bedroom door stood open, jerky silhouettes back-lit by what appeared to be a bedside reading lamp.

The first Chinese to show up in the doorway was a gunner in his early thirties, sporting a suede jacket over a silk shirt and designer jeans. The pistol in his right hand was a shiny Desert Eagle .357 semiautomatic. Just behind him, with one leg in his trousers, and brandishing a pistol, stood a second, younger Triad warrior.

Bolan gave them points for effort. The shooter with the Desert Eagle started blasting at his first glimpse of an adversary, no time wasted on the kind of second thoughts that often got a soldier killed in combat. But his weapon held only ten rounds, and four of those were wasted, going high and wide, before he had a decent fix on Bolan.

And by that time, it was much too late.

The Uzi spit out half a dozen slugs, and Bolan saw his target stagger, lurching back and to his left. The door frame held him for a heartbeat, but his legs had turned to rubber, folding under him. He triggered two more Magnum rounds as he was slumping to the floor, but neither of them came within six feet of Bolan.

Ducking back and out of sight before his comrade fell, the half-dressed gunman fired a shot in Bolan's general direction as he fled. It was too risky to leave him alive and capable of sneaking up on Bolan's blind side. The Executioner knew that he would have to spare the time to do it right.

Reaching underneath his coat, Bolan palmed a frag grenade and dropped the safety pin, baseballing the bomb through the open bedroom door. It didn't matter if the shrapnel scored or not; with any luck, the blast alone should be enough to stun his adversary, giving Bolan time to make the kill.

He crouched, stepped back against the nearest wall and waited for the lethal egg to blow. Five seconds, and it still felt like a lifetime, checking out the upstairs corridor in case the silent rooms hid other gunmen, waiting for a chance to cut him down.

He went in hard behind the blast, smoke in the bedroom swirling like the San Francisco fog outside. A hacking, retching sound led Bolan to his adversary, sprawled beside the bed, still tangled in the trousers he would never have another chance to wear. As the hardman raised his weapon, a short burst from the Uzi finished him, and Bolan turned back toward the stairs.

His nerves were screaming at him, doomsday numbers running in his head, but Bolan took the time to kick that final door and sweep the room that had to be Luk Pang's. There was no one in sight, and he refused to check the closet for a cringing fugitive, when logic told him that his man had to be downstairs, perhaps already fleeing into the darkness.

The Uzi's magazine was almost empty, and he swapped it for a fresh one while on the run. Bolan hesitated fleetingly at the staircase and glimpsed movement below. He had a choice to make. Two more grenades were still clipped to his belt, or he could take the chance and start down on his own, marking each new target as it came.

No choice at all.

He started down the stairs, his Uzi leading. He was ready when a Triad gunner rose from hiding, blasting with a shiny autoloader. One round tugged at Bolan's coat, an almost-hit, before the Uzi stammered its reply and knocked the shooter sprawling, littering his corpse with splinters from the balustrade.

Nobody else was visible as the Executioner reached the ground floor of the town house, glancing backward toward the kitchen, fixing on the front door that was still ajar.

Goddamn it!

Bolan reached the stoop just as a dark sedan sped off, westbound on Fallon, brake lights winking as the driver slowed enough to make the turn on Taylor. At the curb, a second car was busily disgorging gunmen, the same shooters Bolan had already spotted on his drive-by and avoided rousing with his hike across the rooftops.

One of them called out to Bolan, something threatening in Cantonese, and both of them had automatics in their hands. He let his Uzi do the talking, catching the runners with a blazing figure eight that dumped them both on the sidewalk, arms and legs entwined as if they had been cut down in the midst of dancing a waltz.

And it was time to go. Luk Pang had given him the slip, decamped for God knew where. It would require some solid field intelligence to learn if he was fleeing San Francisco or had merely gone to ground. In either case, the Executioner would find no answers standing in the fog and cursing his bad luck while half the neighbors on the block dialed 911.

He passed the first of several squad cars three blocks from the battleground, blue lights flashing. He watched the lawmen go and wished them well.

A soldier's intuition told him that his war lay elsewhere now. If only he could find out where.

5

Vancouver, British Columbia

It was Vancouver. Peter Fong's informed suspicion meshed with hard intelligence from Hal Brognola and the team at Stony Man, one of the Farm's computers spitting out the schedule for a hasty charter flight, northbound from San Francisco less than ninety minutes after Bolan's raid on Fallon Street. Coincidence went out the window when a baggage handler at San Francisco International Airport confirmed the charter passengers had been Chinese.

The choice made sense, of course, on several counts. Aside from Canada's well-known reluctance when it came to extraditing fugitives to the United States, Vancouver offered Luk Pang the kind of sanctuary he would crave just now. The city harbored Canada's single largest concentration of Chinese, many of them known or suspected illegals, and the Triads had connections in Vancouver dating back at least to World War II. An estimated ninety percent of the heroin sold in Canada was China white, imported from the Golden Triangle of Southeast Asia, and most of that came through Vancouver. So did thousands of illegal aliens each year, a fair percentage of them bound for the United States, across a border where restrictions and inspections were lax. Small wonder, then, that British Columbia's heroin addiction rate was five times the Canadian national average, or that certain members of the Royal Canadian Mounted Police had voiced growing concern over the possibility of Asian spies and saboteurs invading western Canada through Vancouver's open door.

Bolan followed Luk Pang's example in regard to transportation, caught a charter flight arranged from Stony Man and touched down at Vancouver International Airport, on Sea Island, at 9:18 a.m. A twenty-something customs officer accepted Bolan's bland assurance that his bags contained no contraband, and Immigration wished him well on his vacation in the province. Once he had his hardware stowed in the rented Toyota Camry, Bolan made his way off-island via South East Marine Drive, winding his way into Vancouver's pulsing heart.

He picked up Cambie Street, northbound, driving around the oasis of Queen Elizabeth Park and across King Edward Avenue, then over False Creek, which separated downtown Vancouver from the Fairview and Mount Pleasant suburbs. Bolan followed the flow of morning traffic on the four-lane bridge, pursuing Cambie Street into the very heart of Chinatown.

At first glance, Bolan entertained the thought that he had driven through a time warp, back to San Francisco and the turf controlled by Sammy Ng. He saw the same bilingual street signs, red-brick buildings in the classic Chinese style, with ornate roofs and hand-carved monsters leering from beneath the eaves. Chinese street markets smelled the same, in Asia or in North America, and self-styled pharmacists still hid their "special" items—including powdered rhinoceros horn and dried tiger's penis—under the counter, away from prying round-eyes.

There were unique points to be seen, as well, but Bolan was no ordinary tourist, fascinated by the sights and smells of Chinatown. He was a hunter, stalking deadly prey on unfamiliar ground. His chances for survival and success were based on hasty preparation, checking into Luk Pang's background and associations, knowing which Vancouver residents he would most likely contact in his time of need.

The red pole—or enforcer—for the local Triad operation, thus equivalent to the lamented Sammy Ng in rank, was Vincent Liu, a Hong Kong native who had immigrated at the age of twenty, back in 1967. If the rumors in Hong Kong were accurate, Liu had already killed at least four men by that time, and his sudden urge to see the world was prompted by investigation into the beheading of a smuggler who had tried to stiff the Triad on its profit from a load of China white. No solid evidence was ever found to justify indictment, and the fact that Liu had never been arrested as an adult cleared the way for him to settle permanently in Vancouver. Ten years later, he was second-in-command of the most powerful crime family in Chinatown. At thirty-three, when cancer claimed his aging boss, Liu took control with no real opposition in the ranks.

As luck would have it, Vincent Liu and Sammy Ng were both affiliated with the Triad known to friends and enemies alike as 14K—a nickname drawn from fourteen-karat gold—which had its roots in Hong Kong, spawning tentacles that reached around the globe. The second largest of nine Triads operating on an international scale, the 14K claimed an estimated membership of twenty-four thousand thieves, smugglers and assassins, scattered among twenty-three regional gangs. In North America, the hotbeds of activity were New York City, San Francisco and Vancouver, but the 14K was also strong in Bangkok and the Golden Triangle, the Philippines, Hawaii, London, and Amsterdam. Investigators from the DEA and Interpol agreed that dealers from the 14K controlled the lion's share of heroin in Western Europe.

And it had also been the 14K—according to Brognola's information, drawn from sources in the CIA and London's MI-6—that cut a devil's bargain with the top dogs in Beijing. When Hong Kong and Macau reverted to the mainland Reds, selected Triad leaders would have earned immunity from government harassment by devoted service to the People's Revolution. Much of it amounted to business as usual—poisoning Americans, Canadians and Europeans with a steady flow of drugs—but "special" favors would be asked from time to time.

Beijing's top agents suddenly had access to the pipeline running aliens from China to the States and Western Europe via Mexico, the Philippines and the Middle East. When China's masters needed military hardware shipped to leftwing rebels in a hurry, anywhere on earth, the Triads could pull strings among their lowlife allies, a rogue's gallery that counted members of the Yakuza, Sicilian Mafia, Colombian cartels and Russian syndicates among its crème de la crime.

The 14K would be his starting point for the Vancouver blitz, and Bolan could imagine no one better to begin with than the godfather himself.

THE CENTERPIECE of Vincent Liu's Vancouver turf was a four-story building just off Pender Street, a hundred yards due west of Shanghai Alley. On the ground floor, Liu maintained a social club where friendly games of fan-tan, dominoes and Chinese checkers were the rule. The second floor was meant to turn a profit, where the classic fan-tan—played with beans, instead of cards, as in the club downstairs—maintained stiff odds in favor of the house, backed up by dice, mah-jongg and a bank of slot machines. Shapely teenaged "hostesses" were standard on the second floor, to keep the losers happy and distract potential winners, and if any guest desired a little horizontal action, he would find it one floor up from the casino—for a price. The building's top floor featured offices and storage space. Its basement, with a separate entrance on the south, away from Pender Street, was Vancouver's most lucrative opium den, catering to a restricted but affluent clientele.

In terms of vice, the Yue-liang Qing—or Moonlight Club—was a browser's paradise, with something for every taste. It had done business at the same address for eighteen years, and had been raided only twice. The first time, someone had been kind enough to telephone ahead and give the Triad time to tidy up the place. When the police returned a second time, a green lieutenant kept the raiding party's destination to himself, scored big with eighty-odd arrests, but it was all in vain. The reigning godfather of Chinatown reminded several ranking cops and city councillors of what might be revealed in public if the case should go to trial. Certain evidence was promptly "lost" and defects were discovered in the affidavit that had gained the police their warrant for the search. All charges were dismissed, and when the confiscated gambling equipment went on sale at auction two weeks later, no one in the audience was fool enough to bid against the elderly Chinese collector seated two rows from the back.

It was the way things worked in Chinatown, and had for better than a century. The white man's law was recognized, acknowledged and selectively ignored. As long as there were no complaints from local businessmen or tourists, nothing in the way of drive-by shootings, corpses in the gutter, the police were satisfied. Youth gangs had become a problem, briefly, but their leaders had been made to see the light when Vincent Liu invited them to dinner at a warehouse on the waterfront. According to pervasive rumors on the street, thirteen young toughs turned up on the appointed night, and nine had gone home sadder and wiser, while four—the "big men" who amused themselves by jeering at Liu over cocktails—took a one-way cruise and wound up feeding game fish in the blue Pacific.

Bolan motored past the Yue-liang Qing and parked near Shanghai Alley, taking care to lock his rented car this time. He still wasn't particularly afraid of thieves, but he didn't like the thought of rushing back in haste and finding one of Liu's assassins in the back seat, armed with a garrote.

Besides, if they pursued him that far, after what he had in mind, the least of Bolan's problems would be fumbling with his car keys.

Walking back in the direction of the club, he breathed the fragrances of Chinatown and noted how its people mostly failed to meet his gaze. A part of that, he guessed, was a conditioned reflex, something taught to Asians in the New World from the cradle up, in days when any sidelong glance directed at a white man was enough to cause offense— which, once upon a time, meant beatings, gunplay, anti-Chinese riots. On the flip side, Bolan speculated, there was bound to be a measure of contempt for round-eyed tourists, with their condescending, racist attitudes that balanced—maybe outweighed—any profit from their cash and credit cards.

If the locals managed to ignore him, all the better. They would have more trouble with descriptions later on, no matter if police or Triad soldiers asked the questions.

Bolan took his time as he approached the Moonlight Club—no rushing that would lead him to mistakes or make the passersby remember him with greater clarity. Beneath the overcoat, the Uzi and Beretta 93-R slapped his sides, while extra magazines for each bulked out his inside pockets. Frag and stun grenades—three each—were clipped to Bolan's belt.

The club's facade was drab compared to others on the block. It had no brightly painted dragons, gargoyles or the like to set it off from neighbors to the east or west. The sign out front was carved in wood, hand-painted, Chinese characters instead of English, but the tourist who mistook the Moonlight Club for one more in a string of shops would either find the door locked or be turned away by some unsmiling Chinese gentleman.

No problem.

There was nearly always more than one way to approach a target, Bolan knew, and he didn't intend to use the front door for his access to the club. Instead, he walked past, continuing two doors farther to an alley on his left. He paused briefly, checking both directions, just to see if he was being watched, before he left the sidewalk, picking up his pace.

The alley was too narrow for Dumpsters, but it had its share of trash cans, neatly capped, with numbers painted on them to identify the shops they belonged to. Maybe it was Canada, or simply Chinatown, but it appeared to Bolan that the trash cans were in better shape than he would normally expect for such a setting in the States—no dents or dings to speak of, no chains tethering the cans to keep a thief from walking off with the previous night's trash. The alley had been overlooked by neighborhood graffiti artists, too. In fact, as Bolan thought about it now, he could recall no evidence of "wall art" vandalism anywhere in *any* Chinatown that he had ever visited.

He reached another alley, running at right angles to the one he was in. It ran between two rows of buildings, back to back, and one of those, away to Bolan's left, was the Moonlight Club. A few more paces, doubling back to the east, brought him to the club's back door.

He took a chance and tried the knob, rewarded by a soft click as it turned.

So far, so good.

He swung the silenced Uzi from underneath his coat and stepped inside.

VINCENT LIU WAS still unclear about the nature of the threat that had unnerved Luk Pang so badly, but he didn't feel like gambling with the empire he had worked so long and hard to build. It was a fact that many Triad soldiers had been killed the night before, in San Francisco, and his latest phone call to the States confirmed that Sammy Ng was now among the dead. So, it seemed, were some of Pang's associates in the political arena, and while Liu despised the Communists, he understood the bargain that his masters had devised, their working treaty with Beijing, and he didn't intend to be the one who earned the Dragon's wrath for spoiling things.

He would cooperate with Luk Pang as much as possible, while protecting himself at the same time. That meant alerting his troops and reinforcing key positions, such as the Moonlight Club, against the possibility of a surprise attack. And *that,* in turn, meant limiting his business for a night or two. But Liu could live with that. It was a waiting game, preventive medicine, and he didn't intend to be caught napping, like his late associate in San Francisco.

There was no denying the attacks that had been made in California, but it wasn't clear to Liu that Luk Pang's enemies hadn't followed him to Canada. There was at least a fifty-fifty chance that they had lost his trail, but those were killer odds, if Liu guessed wrong. Far better to be prepared and arm himself against an enemy that never came than to relax and let some unknown adversary take him unaware.

And part of being safe, he told himself, was looking out for Number One. He couldn't guess how Sammy Ng had let himself be cornered, but the early news said only half a dozen soldiers had been detailed to protect him. That was foolish, if you thought about it—much like using knights and bishops to protect your pawns in chess, while leaving precious king and queen exposed.

In Liu's case he had made directly for his home off Chilco Street, an easy walk from Stanley Park and well removed from Chinatown. Instead of half a dozen guards, he filled the house and wooded grounds with thirty soldiers, mostly new arrivals from the mainland who spoke little English. Never mind. If there was any trouble, they could let their weapons do the talking.

Luk Pang was with him in the spacious house, a nervous-looking man of average height and middle age, who had a problem sitting still. He was forever getting up to peer through the windows, studying the grounds, as if expecting hostile gunmen to attack at any moment. Liu would have commanded that he take a seat, but Pang was still his honored guest, a partner in the Dragon's master plan. If he made trouble in Beijing—or if he had a nasty accident while under the protection of the 14K—there would be hell to pay.

Liu believed that it was practically impossible for anyone from the United States to touch him where he lived. The house was registered in someone else's name, as both a tax dodge and an added measure of security. While Liu wasn't naive enough to think himself invisible, his movements weren't common knowledge, either. Any strangers who came looking for him would begin their search in Chinatown, and they would find no answers there. Just blades and bullets, striking when they least expected it.

Liu almost hoped that someone *would* make an attempt on Pang while he was in Vancouver. It would be a chance for him to show off his soldiers, impress the man whose word meant so much in their business dealings with the Dragon. It was strange, this business of the 14K associating with the mainland Communists, but Liu had quickly recognized the wisdom of the move. With Beijing helping them, the Triads could expand narcotics traffic and secure their bases of operations in Macau and Hong Kong, which would otherwise be swept away within a few short months. The Reds asked little in return—no more than any other business partner would have, less than some—and if there came a day when the regime was swept away, the Triads stood to profit from their long and documented record of resistance.

Had they not cooperated with the CIA in Vietnam, Cambodia, Thailand, the Philippines? It was the Company, not 14K, that had devised the scheme of shipping China white to the United States in U.S. Army body bags.

The British owed a debt of gratitude, as well, for all the times when Triad soldiers had eliminated mainland spies in Hong Kong—even one or two in London, some years back.

Goodwill meant everything in business. It could often see you through where guns and muscle failed...unless, of course, there was a shooting war in progress.

Liu wasn't prepared to guess at who killed Sammy Ng, or why the killers might be stalking Luk Pang. It was disturbing that an enemy would link the two of them, but that didn't mean the collaboration was a failure.

Not just yet.

If it was something local, some dispute in San Francisco's Chinatown, then Liu could put himself at ease. If it turned out to be an international assault, however, he would be prepared for anything.

The answer would reveal itself in time.

All Liu had to do was watch and wait.

IT HAD BEEN TOO GOOD going in, and Bolan cursed himself for kissing off the lesson he had learned so long ago in Special Forces training: Never trust the easy way.

Everybody made mistakes.

Not everyone survived to learn from them.

The first guard, for example, came at him with a knife, when he could just as easily have used a pistol or a shotgun, maybe done the job with one flick of his trigger finger. As it was, he nearly parted Bolan's hair, the Executioner's reaction quick enough to block the slashing downward stroke, as both of them were slammed against the nearest wall.

He got it right the first time, slashing with a knee into his adversary's groin. The blade man staggered, doubled over, gasping in his pain, and Bolan seized the opportunity to drill his skull with three 9 mm rounds at skin-touch range. He didn't have to see the body fall to know he had a kill.

And it was in the fan now, blowing hard and strong, the ripe smell of a setup in his nostrils. He could either try to disengage and scrub the strike, or he could go for broke.

He had about five seconds to decide.

Whatever else was happening around the club this day, it clearly wasn't business as usual. His ears picked up no idle conversation on the ground floor, no busy noises from the kitchen, nothing in the way of tinkling ice cubes, riffling cards or clicking dominoes. There *was* a sudden rush of footsteps on the floor above him, making for the stairs, but in the present circumstances, that was even worse than silence.

Reinforcements.

There was no time for Bolan to think about how his adversaries knew he would be coming, *if* they knew. It was entirely possible that Luk Pang had encouraged his associates to lay strategic traps all over Chinatown on the off chance that he would be pursued from San Francisco into Canada.

Whatever, Bolan knew that he was running out of time.

The next three Triad soldiers came at him with guns, and all at once. He heard them coming from the general direction of the club room, straight ahead, and ducked behind a bulky ice machine that stood in the hallway near the kitchen service entrance. He was quick, but one of them had spotted him and started firing by the time he flattened against the wall.

Two pistols and some kind of lightweight automatic weapon sprayed the corridor from wall to wall and floor to ceiling, bullets drilling through the thin walls of the ice machine and crunching into several hundred pounds of ice cubes in the lower bin. On top, the motor took a string of hits and shorted out, smoke curling from the bullet holes.

It would be suicide to linger where he was and wait for reinforcements to arrive. A few of them were on the stairs already, rushing down to join the fight. Bolan guessed there had to be another way inside the kitchen, which would let them flank him, pop out in the corridor and nail him from behind in a deadly cross fire.

If he didn't make his exit soon, he would lose his chance.

He shoved his SMG around the corner of the ice machine and squeezed off half a dozen rounds with no attempt to aim. One of the Triad gunners fell, and his companions made a dash for cover, both firing as they ran.

There might not be a better time.

The Executioner primed a frag grenade, released the safety spoon to start its countdown, then waited two more seconds for the pitch. At such close quarters, Bolan didn't feel like giving anyone a chance to grab the metal egg and toss it back.

He waited for the blast, three seconds stretching out like thirty in his mind, and when it came, he made his move with jagged shards of shrapnel still in flight. The soldier kept his belly on the floor, pushed off with feet and elbows, crawling toward the club's rear exit while all hell broke loose behind him. Men were screaming back there, others cursing, several firing blindly through a drifting pall of smoke and plaster dust. He reached the door, barged through it, and got to his feet at once.

They would be close behind him, coming fast.

He sprinted back toward the alley that would take him to Pender Street, back to his car. The man who stepped in front of him as the soldier turned the corner was Caucasian, balding, maybe five foot ten. The pistol in his hand was cocked and aimed past Bolan, toward the back door of the club.

"Watch out!" the stranger snapped, unloading four quick rounds almost before the words had passed his lips.

Downrange, the first Triad gunner to clear the doorway went down on his back. The next, a step or two behind him, clutched his side and toppled several trash cans as he fell.

A burst from Bolan's Uzi drove the others back inside—
a temporary respite from the chase. The Executioner's savior made no attempt to stop him as he turned back from the
club and moved toward Pender Street.

"Wait up," the stranger called, as he began to follow
Bolan at a jogging pace. "We need to have a talk. You
drive."

6

"I'd say you're new in town."

There was a note of irony behind the stranger's words, as Bolan drove the Camry east on Hastings, leaving Chinatown behind them.

"You got that right."

"So, let me introduce myself. Brad Phillips, RCMP."

Bolan frowned, but shook the hand that Phillips offered to him. He focused on the traffic that surrounded them, his rearview mirror giving no indication of pursuit.

"We've lost them, never fear," Phillips said.

"Are the Mounties hiring psychics now?"

"Not quite. A logical deduction, Mr....?"

"Blanski," Bolan finished for him. "Mike."

"Mike Blanski, from the States."

In for a penny, Bolan thought, and said, "That's right."

"You're off your range, my friend."

"Not necessarily."

"Let's say the wrong side of the border, then. And hunting out of season, I might add."

"Are you arresting me?"

The question lay between them for a moment, Phillips watching Bolan's profile as he drove, his sharp eyes recording every detail.

"Not just yet."

"May I ask why?"

"Don't tell me you're complaining," the Mountie said. "That's a new one."

"No, but if the shoe was on the other foot and someone blew my stakeout while committing half a dozen major felonies in broad daylight, I'd want to run him in."

"Are you a cop, then?"

"I didn't say that."

"No, I didn't think so. When the Yanks go hunting, most of them respect the border."

"So?"

"The only crimes I've witnessed, so far, are possession of illegal weapons and the discharge of a firearm inside city limits. We can chalk the latter up to self-defense, I'd say. I'm waiting for an explanation, though, before I finish making up my mind."

"I don't believe you followed me to Vincent Liu's," Bolan said, turning south on Jackson Avenue, still driving aimlessly. "That means you had the place staked out, and since we're all alone, it was a one-man job. Some kind of an intelligence assignment, then. Unless I miss my guess, our interests aren't that far apart."

"Our methods vary."

"Not much, from what I saw back in that alley," Bolan stated.

"I couldn't very well stand by and let them shoot you, could I? Not before I had a chance to ask you what in hell is going on."

A sidelong glance showed Bolan that his passenger was smiling. Cautiously, okay, but it was still a smile.

"You're not about to like this," Bolan told him, "but there's only so much I can say."

"In that case," Phillips countered, "let me start. Would it have anything to do with Vincent Liu's connection to a certain fellow Chinese with strong links to Beijing?"

"It may."

"And last night's fireworks down in San Francisco?"

"But you still say you're not psychic?" Bolan asked him.

"Not even close," the Mountie said. "I do watch CNN, though, and it's not that hard to follow up on any points of interest."

"You've been tracking Luk Pang?"

"And Vincent Liu," Phillips replied. "But I really should be asking *you* the questions, shouldn't I?"

"So ask away."

"Who are you, for a start?"

"I told you."

"Not your name," Phillips said. "I'll assume that's temporary, like your transportation. I was really thinking more in terms of *what* you are, who sent you, all that kind of thing."

"I've got a number you can call, in Washington," Bolan said, "but I wouldn't guarantee the answers would do much to satisfy your curiosity. Most likely someone on the other end would want a trade-off, ask to speak with someone higher up."

"It's like that, then?"

"Could be."

"Which means we either cut a deal to let you go your merry way, or raise a stink that does none of us any good at all."

"Two ways to go," Bolan agreed.

"Something tells me you've already come up with a third," Phillips said.

"Maybe. I can't be sure you'll like it."

"Try me out and see."

"We could collaborate," Bolan stated, "to our mutual advantage."

"Hands across the border. That sort of thing?"

"It wouldn't be the first time."

"I should really kick a plan like that upstairs," the Mountie said.

"Whatever you think best."

"In which case, I will more than likely be relieved, while someone else steps in."

"Could happen."

"When I'm the one's been tracking Vincent Liu and company the past two years."

"Fair's fair."

"Damned right," Phillips said, settling back and glaring at the traffic. "Where exactly should we start?"

Washington, D.C.

THE CALL FROM STONY MAN came in on Hal Brognola's private line, the special black phone purring unobtrusively. His scrambler came on automatically, the green light winking at him, indicating that the call was scrambled at the other end.

Precautions.

There was never any letup when it came to physical security around the Farm. The land lines were habitually scrambled, in and out, while any conversations on the radio or cellular phones would be short and cryptic, using a code that was changed each month.

He let the telephone ring twice before he lifted the receiver to his ear. "What's up?" he asked.

The strong, familiar voice of Aaron Kurtzman came back to him through the scrambler. "We just got a call from Striker, in Vancouver," Kurtzman said. "The mark was waiting for him, the way it sounds. He's clear, but it was disappointing for a first contact."

"That's it?"

Brognola wasn't worried about Bolan yet. The man had walked through hellfire time and time again, but somehow it was always Bolan's enemies who wound up getting roasted.

"Ah...there's one more thing," Kurtzman said, sounding hesitant.

"I'm listening."

"He's hooked up with a Mountie somehow."

"Oh?"

It was the only response that came to mind. The big Fed didn't know what kind of trouble Bolan had encountered in Vancouver, and he certainly had no idea how someone from the RCMP figured into it, but he would have to trust the soldier's judgment. One thing he had learned in all his years of picking up the pieces after Bolan blitzed his enemies: you didn't try to second-guess the man.

"We have no indication that the force is formally involved," Kurtzman said. "What I can read between the lines, they're going one-on-one. Some kind of mutual assistance deal."

"My guess would be that Striker knows exactly what he's doing."

"Right. I wonder if he couldn't use some more help, though, to keep things even."

"Help?"

Brognola saw where it was going, but he would let Kurtzman spell it out.

"Um, well, you know that Able Team's tied up right now, that business in Peru."

"So's Phoenix Force," Brognola said. "The Cayman Islands."

"Only three of them. Katz and McCarter are on tap, if you recall."

"You haven't called them yet?" Brognola asked.

"I wanted your okay."

"Let's hold off on the reinforcements for a while," Brognola said. "If Striker's found a local backup he can trust, and he's not asking for assistance, I'd prefer to let him handle it as he sees fit."

"Will do."

"You don't agree?"

"It makes me nervous," Kurtzman admitted grudgingly. "This time out, it's not like he's dealing with some local yokels or a bunch of half-wit terrorists."

"He's never let the side down yet."

"I'd like to keep it that way."

"I'll tell you what," Brognola said. "Let's wait a bit and see how things turn out in Canada. I don't like stepping on the Mounties' toes, if I can help it. Keep the others handy, though, and bring them up to speed on what's been happening. If Striker has to go abroad, we'll let him have some company."

"Affirmative." Relief was audible in Kurtzman's voice.

"That's everything?" Brognola asked.

"So far."

"Okay, then, keep me posted."

"Right."

The line went dead, the scrambler's light winked out and Brognola replaced the handset in its cradle. He considered reaching out to contacts in the Royal Canadian Mounted Police to discover what was happening with Bolan in Vancouver, but he knew enough of the Executioner's style to understand that any deal he might have cut with a specific individual was probably sub-rosa and entirely off-the-record. If he started meddling in the soldier's business now, without a clear fix on the situation, then his effort could be worse than useless. If he blew it, which was likely in the present circumstances, he could put the RCMP onto Bolan's trail, compound the difficulties the man faced already and cause any temporary allies to be busted from their jobs.

No, thank you.

He would wait and see what happened in the next few hours, keep his worries to himself. As for inserting men from Phoenix Force to help out in Vancouver, the big Fed believed it was too late for that. There was at least a fifty-fifty chance that Bolan would complete his business in British Columbia before Brognola had a chance to bring the

Phoenix Force warriors up to speed, and dropping reinforcements on him by surprise was not the best idea, in any
case.

Besides, Brognola knew Vancouver wouldn't be the end
of it. The game was larger than a local Triad family; it
stretched well beyond the continent of North America and
any ChiCom operation running on the continent. The work
wouldn't be done, by any means, when Bolan finished
mopping up around Vancouver.

Later, if he needed help, there would be ample time to use
the men from Phoenix Force as Bolan took his war to other
battlefields. And in the meantime, Kurtzman could be
briefing them, preparing them for what could be the struggle of their lives.

The waiting chafed at Brognola's nerves, but there was no
good way around it. Bolan had to set the pace to suit himself, and it was no good prodding him. You didn't put an
expert in the field with one hand tied behind his back.

Not if you wanted him to win.

Not if you planned on having him survive to fight on another day.

Vancouver, B.C.

BRAD PHILLIPS WONDERED, sometimes, why he never quite
saw trouble coming. It was always like that, on the job and
in his private life. He was a trained professional, with years
of grim, hard-won experience, but stuff was always sneaking up on him, taking him by surprise. The night his wife
had told him she was leaving, for example. Phillips knew
that they were having problems, but he believed that they
could work it out. The news that she was leaving him for
someone else had left him stunned.

Like now, with the American who called himself Mike
Blanski. Never mind that it was almost certainly an alias;
those cloak-and-dagger types all used so many names it had

to be difficult for them to recollect exactly who they really were. Phillips would have used a phony name himself if he had thought about it, but the violence back in Chinatown had shaken him enough that he was just a trifle slower on the uptake than he should have been.

Now, here he was, committed by his own word to assist a total stranger in a flagrantly illegal war against the local 14K and Communist Chinese. He would be lucky to survive the night, and if his supervisors ever found out what he was involved in, he could kiss his job goodbye, perhaps look forward to some prison time on top of blowing off his pension.

His late assignment to observe the Moonlight Club had been a stroke of luck, but only time would tell if it was good or bad. Phillips had managed to convince his captain that he wasn't present when it hit the fan that afternoon—thanks to a one-man stakeout challenging the bowels and bladder more than anything. When he returned from answering the call of nature, Phillips told the brass, there had been gunsmoke in the wind, and he had split before the uniforms arrived to keep from damaging his cover.

That was one good thing about the work in Special Operations: it was handled on a need-to-know priority, and agents working under cover were protected all the way. If that meant marginal participation in a crime, withholding testimony in an unrelated case—whatever—he would have the full support of his superiors. This *other* business, though, well, that was something else.

There was a time, Phillips knew, before he joined the force, when anything could happen. RCMP Special Operations officers weren't above a bit of burglary, illegal wiretapping, whatever was required to make a case, and they could always cover up their tracks as time allowed, when they were done and in the clear. On one occasion, when some radicals from the United States were scheduled for a covert meeting in Quebec, a group of Mounties actually burned the farmhouse where the enemy was scheduled to conduct their rendezvous, and years went by before somebody in the FBI had leaked the story to the press down south.

Those days were gone, of course—at least in theory—and he could expect no mercy if the brass caught him involved in vigilante exercises with a hired gun from America.

What was he thinking of, for God's sake?

Making progress for a change, instead of always sitting on his hands and filing classified reports that wound up under lock and key somewhere, no action taken on the information he provided. It was a heady feeling.

But Phillips knew that he was working without a safety net this time. Deceiving his superiors meant he couldn't reach out for backup if he got in trouble, couldn't count on their support if he was linked to a specific act of violence. They would be forced by law to disavow him, throw him to the wolves—the press and prosecutor's office—if he let himself be caught with dirty hands.

It was too late to change his mind, and that was something of a comfort, after all. It made the rest of his decisions easy, knowing he had passed the point of no return with the first lie to his boss. Everything he said from that point on was suspect, even if he changed his tune and told the whole unvarnished truth. He was committed. The only way for him to go was straight ahead.

If nothing else, at least he had more information now than when he was assigned to shadow Vincent Liu. From Blanski, Phillips had a broader view of what was happening between the 14K and Chinese Communists. He didn't know it all, of course—nor did the tall American, if he was being honest—but the vague conspiracy suspected by the brass had proved out, and it seemed to be a good deal larger, still more sinister, than anyone had bargained for at RCMP headquarters.

It was a strange sensation, knowing more about a case than his superiors. Street cops were often moved around like pawns in chess, kept in the dark on points deemed "sensitive" by those upstairs, sometimes deliberately misled, if high-flown reputations and big money were involved. It didn't always work, of course—the word would often filter down if a "substantial public figure" had been caught red-handed with a teenaged prostitute, or speeding from a drunken hit-and-run, for instance—but a system built on lies, evasions and the like helped undermine the confidence of frontline law-enforcement officers. In special units like the one Brad Phillips served, the need-to-know philosophy was sometimes carried to ridiculous extremes, so that the left hand, literally, often didn't have a clue what the right hand was doing.

It would be a pleasure, Phillips thought, to turn that formula around and have decisions issue from the cop whose life was on the line if anything went wrong, instead of coming from some gray-haired fat cat in an office miles away. He would enjoy it for a change.

As long as the adventure didn't get him killed.

"HOW CAN THIS HAPPEN?" Luk Pang was furious and frightened, all at once, the tremor in his voice betraying him. "How could they trace me here?"

"It all depends on who *they* are," Vincent Liu said. "There must be records of your flight. The pilot was a round-eye, I believe?"

"I used another name," Pang said, aware how lame it sounded even as he spoke.

"Of course." Liu did his best to keep from smirking. "But we have no firm proof that the attack on Yue-liang Qing had anything to do with your arrival in Vancouver."

"I believe it is a logical assumption," Pang replied.

"Indeed. But we repulsed the enemy, and the police seem satisfied with the description of a young street hoodlum bent on robbery. I pointed them in the direction of the Bamboo

Dragons, an annoying group of troublemakers I've intended to dispose of for some time.''

"But he wasn't Chinese, you said."

Liu frowned and shook his head. "A round-eye. Tall, well-armed. A clear description was impossible in the confusion, but we have enough to put the troops on notice. Passersby describe a second man, outside. They are collaborating with a couple of survivors from the club to help create a sketch, as the police do. Even with the tourist traffic, such a man—or men—will find it difficult to pass unnoticed on the streets of Chinatown.''

"You've thought of everything," Pang said with something less than absolute conviction in his tone.

"I know my city," Liu replied. "We have a good relationship with the police, though it was strained this afternoon."

"And if they trace me here?"

"A most unlikely circumstance," Liu said. "But in that case, your enemies will find that they have walked into a hornet's nest, from which there can be no escape."

In truth, Pang knew, the grounds of Liu's estate *were* fortified, within the limits of a model home in one of staid Vancouver's most affluent neighborhoods. There was no razor wire atop the decorative wall that ringed Liu's property, no squad of gunmen out front, but Liu had soldiers in abundance in the house and around the grounds. Closed-circuit cameras watched the street, with someone on the monitors around the clock. It wasn't perfect, but it was the most he could expect on such short notice, in a foreign land.

He didn't want to die.

It startled him a bit to even recognize the thought, with all his talk of sacrifice, the long indoctrination he had undergone from childhood to the day when he received his current mission. Every soldier of the People's Revolution, from the lowest private in the field to reigning politicians in Beijing, was taught to recognize his obligation, willingly accept the fact that he might have to die in order to advance the cause.

Perhaps it was his long exposure to the West, Pang thought, that had begun to weaken his resolve. Attempting to avoid his enemies was only common sense, of course, since he had work to do, but there was all the difference in the world between commitment to survival for the cause and simple fear of death.

Pang didn't feel ashamed of his desire to live, and that was further evidence of his corruption. If his masters in Beijing could look inside his brain and read his thoughts, they would have packed him off to a reeducation camp without delay. Weak links made useless chains, and any soldier who would place himself, his own safety, above the bold objectives of his leaders, could be a potential traitor.

But that was ridiculous. Luk Pang had served the People's Revolution all his life—almost from birth, in fact, when he was taken from his parents, to the state-run training school. He never questioned his superiors. It was *himself* he doubted, and the weakness that had surfaced in the past twelve hours, when his own mortality was driven home by faceless men who stalked him like an animal.

Survival was the top priority, he told himself, and not because he had an urge to live, sip wine and whiskey to his heart's content and make love to women on a bed with satin sheets. It was because the People's Revolution *needed* him alive, to follow through on his assignment from Beijing. The Dragon needed him to carry out the next phase of their plan.

And he could serve the cause by finding out exactly who his adversaries were, obtaining prisoners if possible and finding out how much they knew. Assuming capture was impractical, the next best thing was to annihilate his enemies before they had a chance to further interrupt a scheme so vast and noble it would lie beyond their small ability to comprehend.

He would survive, Luk Pang thought, because he had to. He owed it to his country and his people.

Survival was the best revenge, and Luk Pang would see his adversaries slaughtered yet. This time tomorrow, or the next day, he looked forward to the opportunity of pissing on their graves.

7

The bank on Hastings Street wouldn't be found in the business listings of the Vancouver telephone directory. There was no impressive edifice, no sign out front or advertisement in the daily newspapers to lure new depositors. In fact, the whole idea was to avoid the kind of customers who walked in off the street with several hundred dollars in a purse or wallet, looking for someplace to open up a small account.

This bank was owned and operated by the 14K, for Triad business only. In a given year, some thirty million dollars might be funneled through the unassuming redbrick building, cash from drugs and other outlaw enterprises reinvested in the market, stocks and bonds, or cycled back through Chinatown by means of off-the-record loans to needy businessmen. The banks selected customers were scrupulous about repaying any moneys owed, along with interest averaging some forty-five percent, compounded weekly. They didn't complain to the authorities and rarely missed a payment, knowing from experience what the result would be if precious confidentiality wasn't preserved.

Officially the business was a pawnshop, and it turned a dollar on that end, as well, but nothing like the millions that were counted, stacked and stashed in back, stuffed into duffel bags and suitcases, packed off to safe deposit boxes, lawyer's offices or westbound flights to Hong Kong. Vincent Liu was the de facto owner of the bank, though he was rarely seen about the premises. Thus far, no paper trail had been discovered that would leave him open to a charge of tax evasion. The investigation was continuing, Brad Phillips said, but going nowhere fast.

Mack Bolan, on the other hand, had no need for a warrant or subpoena when he strolled into the pawnshop, leaving Phillips in the rental car outside. It was a one-man job, and he preferred a smooth, swift getaway to having someone watch his back inside the bank.

The middle-aged proprietor was smiling as he came to greet his unexpected round-eyed customer. The Uzi wiped away his smile and markedly improved his grasp of English in the length of time it took for him to understand that playing dumb could get him killed. He led his unexpected visitor behind a chest-high wooden counter, through a cluttered storage area and upstairs to the counting room.

There was a lookout on the door, all frowns as Bolan and the pawnbroker came up the stairs. There was no telling what it was that passed between them—possibly a look, perhaps a hand sign Bolan couldn't see—but he was ready when the young Chinese sidestepped and reached inside his jacket, going for the pistol he kept hidden there. At the same time, the pawnbroker turned back and tried to clear the field of fire, his progress halted by the hand that gripped his scrawny throat.

The Uzi locked on target, stuttering a 6-round burst that sounded more like canvas ripping than a blast of automatic gunfire. Parabellum manglers took the sentry down before he reached his weapon, dumping him in a corner near the unmarked door he was assigned to guard.

"You're running out of chances," Bolan told the small man wriggling in his grasp. A light touch from the Uzi's muzzle emphasized the point.

"Okay."

The door was locked, but Bolan's escort gave a coded knock and waited while the latch was opened from inside. Before the doorman could recover from the shock of seeing two men on the threshold, one of them a round-eye, Bolan caught him with a flying kick that threw the door back in his face and knocked him on his ass. The tough guy tried to reach his sidearm, and a short burst from the Uzi nailed him to the floor.

That left two older men in business suits and a young woman, all engaged in bundling stacks of currency before the sight of Bolan and the dead man at his feet froze them like statues where they sat. Assuming they spoke English, he addressed them directly.

"I'll be making a withdrawal—all the money you can fit inside that suitcase over there. Start with the large bills first, and hold the singles back for last."

They hesitated, staring at him, until he fired another short burst at the ceiling and the woman gave a breathless little scream. One of the men got up and fetched the suitcase, and they collaborated on the packing, making tidy stacks and rows. When they were done, Bolan estimated there was something like $800,000 in the bag. The smaller bills, still heaped up on the table, would have easily made another quarter million.

"You'd better go now," Bolan told them, nodding toward the door. "I guess you didn't hear the fire alarm."

He palmed a slim incendiary stick, struck the fuse, dropped it on the table piled with currency and turned to follow them downstairs. Before he reached the sidewalk, they had vanished, lost among their fellow countrymen.

"Lost luggage?" Phillips asked him, as he tossed the suitcase in the car's back seat.

"My war chest," Bolan replied. "The 14K insisted on a generous donation."

"Wonders never cease," the Mountie said, and he was laughing as he pulled out into traffic, headed west.

THE BEST WHOREHOUSE in Chinatown was found on Seymour Street, near Dunsmuir. Brad Phillips knew the place from discussions with Vancouver vice detectives and poring over RCMP files that detailed operations of the Triad known as 14K. According to the various reports that he had read, the brothel's clientele was almost evenly divided between Occidentals and Chinese, the former being mostly local businessmen and "civic father" types, together with some wealthy tourists in the know about Vancouver's seamy side. The Asians who spent time there, likewise, were among the economic upper crust. With prices starting at two hundred dollars for an hour, your average working stiff of any race would have to seek his relaxation elsewhere.

Phillips parked the Camry on a side street and turned to face his companion while the man was checking out his gear. "I'm going in this time," the Mountie said.

"It's not a good idea."

"Why not? You think the force will take it easy on me if I only drive getaways?"

"Two men inside, it's twice as likely one of us will stop a bullet," Bolan told him.

"Half as likely, I'd say, if you've got someone to watch your back."

They were already wasting time, and Bolan shrugged in acquiescence. "Suit yourself. You take the back door, right?"

"Suits me."

The alley smelled like fish and cabbage. Phillips concentrated on his destination, had the Browning semiautomatic pistol in his right hand as he tried the doorknob with his left. It turned, and the door swung inward, well-oiled hinges giving him an edge.

The man who stood before him with a plastic bag of garbage in each hand looked startled. He was on the verge of bolting, shouting an alarm, when Phillips stuck the pistol in his face.

"I wouldn't, friend."

"Who are you?"

"Pest control," Phillips replied. "Turn around and keep your mouth shut, if you know what's good for you. Let's join your friends."

They traveled ten or fifteen yards along a murky corridor, with sounds of all-male conversation drawing closer by the step, before his grudging escort swung one of the garbage bags, releasing it, contents exploding in the Mountie's face.

He fired twice and saw the running figure stumble, go down on his face, the second trash bag wedged beneath him. Down the hallway someone shouted in alarm, and Phillips heard them coming for him, half a dozen by the sound.

There was no cover for him in the hallway proper, and he tried the first door on his left, checking out the smallish storage room. Nobody home. Twelve rounds remained in his pistol, and he had two spare magazines of thirteen each. He simply hoped it was enough.

He peered around the doorjamb, saw a muzzle-flash and answered it with two rounds of his own before the angry bullets started spraying plaster dust and splinters in his face.

The enemy could pin him down and rush the door, or simply creep in close enough so that next time Phillips stuck his face around the corner, he would find the muzzle of a gun pressed to his forehead. They could even wait and starve him out, if they had time, but he supposed the raucous sounds of gunfire would impart a need for haste.

No matter how he tried to break it down, his situation was unfortunate at best, hopeless at worst.

Phillips was as shocked by the explosion as the Chinese in the corridor outside his hiding place, but he was covered from the storm of shrapnel.

They weren't.

He heard them screaming, gagging on the smoke, and poked his head around the corner, following his pistol. Three of them were down, two others slumped against the walls and clutching bloody wounds. The Mountie finished them with two quick shots, deciding he would rather live with burdens on his conscience than be worm food in the grave.

Another figure was approaching through the pall of smoke and dust. He had the pistol braced in both hands when a deep, familiar voice reached out to him.

"It's me," Bolan said. "I've set incendiaries. Time to go."

"The women?"

"None around that I could find. Looks like another setup. They were waiting."

Not too long, though, Phillips thought, as he moved toward the exit, back along the alley, to the street where they had parked the rental car.

He had seen more death and destruction in the past two hours than he had in the sixteen years of his career to date. A part of Phillips told him he should be appalled, guilt-ridden, but another voice advised the first one to shut up.

He slid behind the Camry's steering wheel, unlocking his companion's door from the inside. Amazingly there was no tremor in his voice as he inquired, "Where next?"

"WE NEED MORE SOLDIERS," Vincent Liu proclaimed. "More guns. See to it!"

His lieutenants glanced at one another apprehensively, before the eldest of them, David Chung, spoke up. "Our men are all on duty now," he said. "There are no more."

Liu turned to glare at Chung, his scowl encompassing the others. "What? How is that possible?"

"Your orders were—"

"I know the orders that were given! Do you take me for a senile idiot?"

"No, sir."

"How many dead and wounded is it now?" Liu asked of no one in particular.

"Nine dead, six wounded," Michael Lau replied. From the expression on his face, he instantly regretted having spoken.

"Fifteen men!" Liu felt the hot blood rushing to his face. "And we don't even know the enemy by name, or how many are involved!"

"Two men, at least," said William Chow, the third of Liu's lieutenants. "We've confirmed that with survivors from both incidents."

"Two men. Two *white* men, moving as they please through Chinatown and slaughtering my soldiers everywhere they go! We need patrols out on the street to track them down. There is no time to waste!"

"But we were told—"

Liu's glare cut off the rest of Lau's remark. "To protect our major operations first, I know. When I gave those instructions, there were still doubts in my mind that we would be attacked at all. I hoped the problem might be limited to San Francisco, but we've seen that I was wrong."

The three lieutenants blinked in unison at their master's frank admission of an error. It was better than a screaming tantrum, but it worried them, as well. If Vincent Liu had doubts about himself, their situation had to be grave indeed.

"The time has come to reevaluate our strategy," Liu said. "Instead of simply waiting for the enemy to strike at us, we must be more aggressive, track down our adversaries and wipe them out before they damage us irreparably."

"Where should we start?" Chung asked.

"Our friends at the police department may know something," Liu replied. "If not, perhaps we can encourage them to organize their efforts more effectively." He cracked a smile and said, "We are taxpayers, after all."

The three lieutenants laughed obligingly, with no real mirth behind it, waiting for their master to continue. When Liu spoke again, the smile had vanished from his face.

"If the police can't help us, we must do the job ourselves. It is impossible to search Vancouver, but we own the streets of Chinatown. Reach out to every contact in the district. I want everyone alert to strangers. These men won't be easily confused with tourists. Anyone suspicious should be instantly reported. I want soldiers ready to respond upon a moment's notice. Have one team wait at Victory Square, the other at Blood Alley, where they can respond to any point in Chinatown without delay. Six men per team to start, and they can call for reinforcements if they feel the need."

"It shall be done," Chung said.

"And while you're at it, tell the men there is a bounty on the round-eyes. Shall we say five thousand dollars each?"

"The soldiers will be pleased," Lau replied. "It is most generous."

"I want them shooting straight and hitting what they aim at. We cannot afford mistakes."

Dismissing his lieutenants with a wave, Liu poured himself a glass of whiskey, drank it down and scowled at the idea of facing Luk Pang. It couldn't be avoided, but he dreaded the inevitable confrontation. Pang was bound to criticize his methods, and Liu had no answer for him yet, not while the round-eyes were at liberty to roam the streets of Chinatown and massacre his men.

But that would change, and swiftly. Liu couldn't allow himself to be humiliated in the eyes of peasants. It was bad for business, and he had to wash that shame away.

With blood.

IT WAS AN HONOR being chosen for the strike team, Sansan Chien decided, even if it placed him in more danger than the troops assigned to guard specific targets. Greater risk meant great reward, if he could only be the one who brought the round-eyes down. A simple shot was all he asked for, and five thousand dollars in his pocket when the smoke cleared.

Easy.

All they had to do was find the round-eyes, then corner them and finish off the job before police arrived.

And, somehow, keep from being shot down in the process.

The mobile phone beside him chirped its trilling call, and Chien responded on the first ring, listened briefly, smiling as he dropped it back onto the seat.

"Let's go," he told the driver. "Two white men with guns just walked into the Yang-rou Social Club on Dunsmuir Street. We've got them, if we hurry."

Acceleration pressed Chien back into his seat as they burned rubber, screeching from the curb. As he checked the Ingram submachine gun in his lap, he wondered if the other team would get a summons from Blood Alley. Hopefully they would be left to watch for any other enemies who might turn up while Chien and his four soldiers nailed the trouble down.

Two round-eyes meant ten thousand dollars if he bagged them both. As leader of the team, Chien calculated he should keep five thousand for himself and split the rest among his men. They should be grateful for the chance to share in his benevolence. Where would they be without him, after all, but staking out some cutting plant or whorehouse, waiting for the enemy to take them by surprise.

It was a short run to the social club, but Chien and his commandos almost missed their targets, even so. A bus pulled out in front of them and wasted precious moments, Chien gesticulating at the driver, shouting Chinese curses, until they finally found room to pass it on the right. As they approached the club, Chien saw the round-eyes driving off in a Toyota, one of them still firing at the club while Triad soldiers scattered, diving for the pavement.

A loud explosion rocked the club as Chien's car pulled abreast, his driver swerving, startled by the shock wave, bricks and shrapnel cast into the street.

"Catch up to them!" Chien shouted, rolling down his window even as he spoke. He leaned out with the Ingram, squinting in the rush of wind, and tried to draw a bead on the Toyota.

Damn! The round-eye at the wheel was swerving like a drunken maniac, across three lanes. Oncoming vehicles were forced to veer aside to avoid a collision. Chien gave up on the idea of a precision shot and held down the Ingram's trigger, unloading half the magazine in one long burst. Spent brass rained on the street behind them, bouncing musically across the asphalt.

"Did you hit them?" Chang Loo shouted at him from the back seat, craning forward.

"Quiet!"

Even as he barked the order, Chien was squeezing off another burst of automatic fire. This time he saw a couple of his bullets strike the Camry's trunk, but that was all. For all he knew, the other dozen rounds were wasted.

"Get me closer, damn it!"

While the driver did his best to carry out the order, Chien retrieved a fresh mag from the glove compartment and reloaded, thankful that he didn't fumble with it while his men were watching. They were almost on the Camry's bumper when he craned back out the window, aiming for a kill. He couldn't fail to hit the driver this time, if he only—

Damn!

The target vehicle swung hard off to the left, its driver braking simultaneously, so that Chien and company were on the verge of passing it before they could react. Chien saw a round-eyed gunman swivel toward him, in the shotgun seat, a bulky-looking weapon thrust out through his window.

"Wait! Look out!"

Too late, Chien's driver saw the peril, groping for his own brake pedal as the enemy's submachine gun stitched a line of holes across their windshield, pebbled safety glass cascading into Sansan's lap. A white-hot ice pick pierced

Chien's shoulder, nailed him to the seat, and something sticky splashed onto his face before the headless driver slumped into his lap. Chien saw the bank of gaily painted storefronts rushing toward him, registered that they were still accelerating, somehow, as he found the strength to scream.

THEY HAD BEEN LUCKY with the Camry. Two rounds had drilled into the trunk and one grazed the left rear fender. Phillips stopped at a convenience store and bought a can of spray paint that was close enough to pass a casual inspection, using just enough to hide the shiny steel where paint had flaked away on impact. It would never fool a cop—or anybody else, up close—but it would do for the time being, in a major city where ignoring strangers and their vehicles was the norm.

"Too close for comfort," Phillips said, when they were on the road again.

"You were expecting comfort?" Bolan asked.

"Let's just say I was hoping to survive the afternoon."

"You're halfway there."

"That's comforting. Where are we off to now?"

"Are you familiar with the Shan-dian Club?"

"You mean the gambling house on Hamilton?"

"The very same."

Their target stood within the shadow of Vancouver Community College, still a part of Chinatown, another of the "social clubs" that hid illegal gaming halls behind a thin veneer of simple camaraderie. They sat outside and watched the place for several minutes, saw nobody passing in or out through the ornate doors.

"Another setup?" Phillips offered.

"Would you be surprised?"

The Mountie shook his head. "I've never seen the quarter buttoned down this way before. If nothing else, you've put a crimp in poor old Vincent's business."

"It's a start," Bolan said, "but I still want Luk Pang."

"If I were him," Phillips replied, speculating, "I'd lay up at Liu's place, out by Stanley Park."

"It's on my list," the Executioner told him, "but I'd prefer to wait for dark. Shall we proceed?"

"Why not? I hate to keep the little buggers waiting."

"Front or back?"

"I'll take the front this time. Might flash the tin, if they get nasty."

"Just so no one gets your number."

"No one who'll be giving it away," Phillips said with a tight-lipped smile.

They crossed the street together, separating at the sidewalk, Bolan moving swiftly down one of the carbon-copy alleys that were everywhere in Chinatown. More garbage cans, the same aroma he had grown accustomed to by now, a scuttling cat that fled the field without a backward glance.

The back door of the Shan-dian Club was locked, and Bolan spent a moment with his picks to beat the tumblers, cursing at the image of Brad Phillips going in without him, mixing with the Triad troops before his backup had arrived. As if in answer to his thoughts, a burst of shots rang out as the Executioner cleared the door and moved along a hallway lit by naked bulbs at ten-foot intervals.

In front of him, three gunners suddenly appeared in answer to the sounds of combat, missing Bolan as they turned and ran in the direction of the gaming club's main room. He wasted no time on a warning call, unleashing the Uzi with a searing burst that swept the three of them from left to right and dropped them squirming in their tracks.

So much for overconfidence.

He charged along the corridor, following the sounds of combat to the large room where the gamblers normally convened to watch their savings melt away. No players were on hand this afternoon, just Triad soldiers who had obviously been assigned to wait for someone to show up and try to bust the place. Brad Phillips had already gotten past the doorman, clearing the hurdles that would block your average civilian coming off the street, but six or seven gunners had been waiting for him in the main casino.

Phillips was pinned down as Bolan entered, crouched behind a roulette table he had tipped to give himself some cover. It was working, to a point, but solid wood could only take so much, in terms of bullets striking home from forty feet or less. He would be running low on ammunition and running out of time, unless he got some help.

The silencer on Bolan's Uzi, coupled with the racket from their own guns, kept the Mountie's enemies from recognizing danger at their backs. When the soldier came upon them, five were clearly visible, with nothing in the way of cover, and he wasted no time cutting loose with everything he had. So focused were they on the adversary right in front of them, that three had fallen in a hail of parabellum rounds before the others recognized the mortal danger on their flank.

Too late.

Two gunners turned and tried to get a fix on Bolan, crouching in the shadows, but he dropped them both with short bursts from his SMG. The others panicked, bolting without any thought of how they would escape, where they would go, and the casino was transformed into a slaughterhouse. As Bolan raked the room with automatic fire, Phillips rose from cover, pumping hot rounds from his Browning into anything that moved.

It took them all of forty seconds, mopping up. The room smelled heavily of blood and cordite when they finished, bodies scattered on the floor in spreading pools of crimson, fancy wallpaper and ornate furnishings all shot to hell.

They went out through the front together, brushing past a gaggle of Chinese pedestrians attracted to the sounds of gunfire. Someone would remember them, of course, and that was fine. If they saw fit to speak with the police, descriptions would be vague, the next best thing to useless. Triad soldiers might be more successful in extracting information from their fellow countrymen, and that was fine with Bolan, too.

He wanted Vincent Liu and Luk Pang to know that Death was coming for them, and he hoped that both of them would stand and fight. It would be easier that way.

But he would take it any way it came.

8

Luk Pang had heard enough. He understood why Vincent Liu was anxious for him to remain in town—to give Liu another chance to prove himself—but that wasn't Pang's problem. At the moment, he had more important issues on his mind.

Like trying to survive another night.

Liu's plan had started to unravel almost from the start. It sounded great in theory, shutting down the major businesses in Chinatown and manning them with soldiers while they waited for the enemy to strike and so ensnare himself. Pang had been hopeful at the outset, but it simply didn't work.

They could debate Liu's failure endlessly—was he outnumbered by the round-eyes, were his soldiers negligent or unprepared?—but Luk Pang didn't possess the luxury of time. He had already seen what happened in San Francisco, when he lingered in the charnel house and left himself exposed. This day, the pattern was repeating itself in Vancouver, and the best thing he could do was get away before his unknown adversaries had another chance to take him out.

New York was waiting for him. He had called ahead, explained his problem to the men in charge of Chinatown. A second call instructed his own troops to get ready, just in case. New York would put three thousand miles between himself and those who stalked him. By the time they traced him there, if that was even possible, Luk Pang would have his personal defenses ready. No one would survive if they came after him in New York City.

Walking to the helipad with Vincent Liu beside him, Pang couldn't deny his confidence was shaken. Being hounded from two cities in as many days was a humiliating circumstance, and one his mainland masters wouldn't understand. He hadn't spoken to them of the violence in Vancouver, yet, preferring to reserve that ordeal for another time, when he was safely in New York. The Dragon would be angry at the disruption of their plans, but it wasn't a fatal setback.

Not so far.

Pang had to find out who was stalking him and put an end to it. In San Francisco he had let himself believe that it came down to Sammy Ng, some problem on the red pole's turf that would evaporate once Ng had been replaced. Instead, the plague had followed Pang across the border into Canada. His enemies had been revealed as round-eyes, and there could be no doubt they were stalking *him,* along with everyone he touched.

So, it was time to run. Again. And for the last time, Pang decided. He would make his stand in New York City, pull out all the stops to finally destroy his nameless enemies. If nothing else, at least he had to identify the men who hunted him and warn the Dragon, so that other members of the team could take precautions, guard themselves against attack.

The Hughes 500 four-man helicopter waited for him, engine idling, rotors turning sluggishly. Pang shook the hand Liu offered to him, wished the man luck and climbed into the chopper's cockpit. Moments later he was airborne, watching figures on the ground grow smaller, shrinking into toys, then insects, as they turned and flew south toward the airport.

It was good to be in motion once again. This time, with any luck, his problems would be left behind him for a while.

BOLAN WATCHED the helicopter circle once above the house and grounds, then level off and make a beeline southward. Going where? The airport would be logical, and there was no way he could catch Pang now, not even if he scrubbed the raid on Vincent Liu, called Phillips off and ran back to his waiting car.

Another miss, damn it, but the effort didn't have to be a waste of time. Luk Pang was one of Bolan's targets in Vancouver, but he also meant to bring down the local Triad, or leave it in such disarray that power struggles in the ranks would keep the Chinese gangsters busy for a while, as law enforcement sifted through the rubble.

Vincent Liu was still at home, and he was still on Bolan's hit list, coming up at Number One with a bullet.

It was dark out, and the Executioner had swapped his street clothes for a combat blacksuit under military webbing. His M-16 A-1 assault rifle carried an M-203 grenade launcher slung below its barrel and was fitted with a 100-round drum magazine. Twin bandoliers—one for grenades, the other fat with spare mags for the rifle—crisscrossed Bolan's chest. He wore the sleek Beretta 93-R underneath one arm, with a semiautomatic Desert Eagle .44 Magnum riding his hip. The belt around his waist held reloads for the pistols, plus a mix of hand grenades, including smoke, frag and incendiaries. He also carried a Ka-bar fighting knife and a wire garrote.

Something for everyone.

He had approached Liu's mansion from the north, a long jog through the park from where his car was parked on Comox Street, while Phillips worked his way in from the south. The property was surrounded by a wall, perhaps constructed with security in mind, but it wasn't enough to stop determined soldiers. There would be sentries on the grounds, but it was mostly dark, except for floodlights splashing glare around the house and backyard helipad.

He could have tried to nail the chopper, maybe lobbed a 40 mm high-explosive round from hiding, at the outer limits of effective range, but Bolan let it go. A wasted shot would throw away whatever slim advantage he possessed from coming at his adversaries by surprise.

They were expecting him—expecting *someone,* from the look of things—but there was still an attitude, perhaps a hope, that Liu's estate wouldn't be touched by the explosive violence that had shaken Chinatown. It was supposed to be his sanctuary, where the red pole could relax, forget about his troubles for a while, let others deal with hassles on the street.

The godfather of Chinatown had learned to delegate authority, let others take his lumps whenever possible, but he couldn't escape the heat this time. His tab was coming due, and Bolan wouldn't leave without collecting on the overdue account. He started forward, edging toward the light.

As Bolan reached the tree line, Liu, flanked by a pair of bodyguards, was reentering the house, some ninety yards away. The shot was well within his launcher's certified effective range, and the Executioner took a chance, aimed high and sent a high-explosive round across the lawn to herald his arrival. It missed the door where Liu had disappeared by half a foot or less, exploding in a smoky thunderclap that punched a new hole in the wall.

Before the first concussive echo of the blast had died away, Bolan was on his feet and sprinting toward the house, reloading the grenade launcher as he ran. A buckshot round, this time, would greet the soldiers who were just emerging from the shadows on the east side of the house, responding to the noise of the explosion. Two of them had Bolan spotted, pointing, calling to their fellows.

Bolan squeezed the M-203's trigger from a range of twenty yards. It gave the buckshot ample room to spread, a storm of .33-caliber projectiles ripping through the palace guard, dropping several of them in their tracks, the others reeling, wounded, dazed or frightened. The M-16 A-1 spoke up to finish them, a waist-high burst of 5.56 mm tumblers flattening survivors of the buckshot blast.

The fat was in the fire now; there could be no turning back.

He poured on the speed, rushing toward the house.

BRAD PHILLIPS HEARD the first grenade go off as he was edging closer to the front of the house, where several high-priced cars were lined up in the driveway. He was better armed this time: the Uzi submachine gun, with its silencer detached, to supplement his Browning, and the hand grenades suspended from his belt.

It was like playing war, he'd thought, when they were suiting up back at the car, but it wasn't a game. Men had been dying all day long, and more were being killed this very minute, out of sight, behind the house. There would be murder charges waiting if his name was ever linked to this night's work.

Assuming he survived.

The helicopter taking off had worried him, made Phillips wonder if their targets were escaping, but there was no word from Blanski on the little two-way radio he carried, nothing to suggest that they were pulling back.

The explosion was his signal, bringing Phillips out from under cover of the hedge where he had lain since creeping through the trees and darkness, eighty yards from where he'd scaled the outer wall to penetrate Liu's fortified preserve. The cars were just in front of him, two drivers lounging up against a gray Mercedes-Benz when the explosion made them drop their cigarettes and reach for side arms. They weren't among the group who sprinted toward the rear, however. Someone had to stay and watch the cars.

He came up on their blind side, closed the gap to six or seven yards before he had to make the choice. It ran against the grain for him to simply shoot them in the back, but Phillips didn't want the goons to kill him, either. So he compromised: a subtle clearing of his throat, enough to capture their attention, start them turning back in his direction as he squeezed the Uzi's trigger. Parabellum slugs dropped both men on the asphalt, side by side.

He ran around the Benz, made sure those two were dead and had a fair start up the front steps to the house when two more gunmen crossed the threshold, breaking left and right as soon as they had room. One, on his left, was leveling a stubby riot shotgun, while the other had an automatic pistol in his hand.

Phillips had been taught that a shotgun was the more dangerous of the two weapons, the spray of pellets making lethal hits more likely, even when your adversary was a poor marksman. Pistols, on the other hand, required at least a nod toward taking aim, unless the muzzle was in contact with the target when you fired.

The Uzi stuttered, spewing brass and bullets, spinning the shotgunner like a giant weather vane. His buckshot charge took out one of the floodlights somewhere overhead, and cast a portion of the front porch into sudden gloom.

There was enough light for the second gunman, though, and Phillips sidestepped, dropping to a crouch as bullets started snapping past him in the night. He held down the Uzi's trigger and swept the porch, aware that he was wasting ammunition, still preferring that to going down without a fight. In fact, the long burst seemed to rattle his opponent, made the shooter duck and flinch, threw off his aim, and by the time he made an effort to recover, parabellum rounds were ripping through his chest and torso, blowing him away.

The tall front doors stood open, waiting to receive him. Phillips rushed the steps and barged across the porch, past dead men twitching in their pools of blood, then cleared the threshold in a crouch.

He was inside.

Now all he had to do was find Luk Pang or Vincent Liu, kill one or both of them—and anyone who tried to stop him in the meantime.

Simple.

The hard part would be getting out alive.

THE CARPET TASTED DUSTY, even though Liu knew it had been vacuumed the previous day. It took a moment, in his daze from the explosion, for the master of the house to understand that dust was raining upon him from the ceiling. Hands clasped his arms and dragged him to his feet, but he was still disoriented and unstable, shaken by the blast so close at hand.

With the explosion ringing in his ears, Liu barely heard the gunfire from the yard, but he was hustled down a spacious hallway by his bodyguards and into his library. The room was free of windows, with shelves of books from floor to ceiling on all sides. A sniper couldn't reach him from outside.

"What's happening?" Liu asked the older of his watchdogs, clutching at the gunman's arm.

"I don't know, sir."

"Well, find out, damn it! Stop this madness. Kill the man who dares attack my home!"

The soldiers left him, but he knew that one of them would be on guard outside the door, unless Liu ordered him to leave. Their most important duty was to keep the red pole safe from harm, at any cost. The U.S. Secret Service could have taken lessons from his soldiers, when it came to dedication and a willingness to die for honor's sake.

A second powerful explosion rocked the house, this time at the rear. His ears had cleared enough to hear the gunfire now, still muffled by a maze of intervening walls, but loud enough to let him know he was in mortal danger. Trembling, Liu moved toward his antique teakwood desk, unlocked the upper right-hand drawer and took out his favorite pistol.

It wasn't much, compared to what he heard outside—the automatic weapons and explosives—but it was the best he could do on such short notice. Liu had counted on his soldiers to protect him, never giving much thought to what would happen if he had to stand and fight alone.

Six years had passed since he killed a man with his own hands, but Liu hadn't forgotten how. He still remembered clearly how it felt to point a gun and pull the trigger, feel the recoil in his wrist and forearm, watch the human target crumple like a broken mannequin. He had enjoyed that feeling, once upon a time, and would again.

The pistol was a Walther P-5 semiautomatic, double-action, fully loaded with an 8-round magazine and one round in the chamber. Liu felt no compulsive need to check it, knowing he had loaded it himself and kept the weapon under lock and key. The fact that someone sought to kill him wasn't enough to make Liu doubt himself, his memory, his senses.

Feeling better with the pistol in his hand, he poured himself a glass of brandy, drank it at a swallow and refilled the glass. Outside, the sounds of battle were increasing, and it seemed to Liu that he could now hear gunfire echoing inside the house.

He drained the brandy glass, set it aside and hurried to the door. One of his soldiers waited in the hall outside, as Liu expected.

"Come with me!" Liu ordered, turning to his right and moving toward the parlor, which in turn would bring him to his own front door, the driveway and the vehicles that would permit him to escape. The worried-looking soldier hastened to keep up.

Immediately Liu smelled cordite, faint at first, but un- mistakable to anyone who ever fired a weapon. That, and something else. A fire?

As if in answer to his thought, a nearby smoke alarm be- gan to screech, its warning echoed automatically by others in the house. Their hellish noise gave Liu an instant head- ache, set his teeth on edge, but there was nothing he could do to shut them down. He had no time to spend on trifles, when his life was hanging in the balance.

Glancing back, in the general direction of the earlier ex- plosions, Liu could see the smoke now. He could stand and watch his great house burn, if he was so inclined, but the survival instinct kept him moving, with the youthful sol- dier on his heels. More gunshots erupted ahead of him, sounding like the fireworks children lit for Chinese New Year. Overhead, the lights began to flicker.

Liu reached back to grab his soldier's arm and propelled the young man in front of him. There was no need to warn him of potential danger. They were moving through a war zone, and the guard's job was to walk before his master, clear the path of enemies.

The red pole cursed the young man when he stumbled and lost his footing, reeling against the left-hand wall. It took another heartbeat for Liu to decipher what had happened, to see the crimson smears across the plaster as the gunner slumped and died.

The lights went out.

Liu dropped into a prone position, both hands wrapped around the Walther as he thrust it out in front of him. A man was moving toward him, coming closer. He was just a silhouette, until he fired a short burst from his submachine gun. In the brief light of the muzzle-flash, Liu saw the stranger was a white man.

It was all he had to know.

The Walther cracked four times, and Liu was instantly rewarded as his target staggered, then fired a short burst at the ceiling as he fell. His weapon lay between them, separated from its owner by a critical three feet as Liu stood and moved past his adversary, making sure to keep him covered all the way.

It was a waste of time.

A few more yards and he would be outside, several cars waiting for him. Liu could take his pick, drive out of there and leave his soldiers to the cleanup detail. If police arrived before they finished, he could always have a private word with friends at headquarters. Some kind of meeting would now be necessary, in any case.

But first he had to save himself.

And from the noise still audible behind him, he was running out of time.

A WILD ROUND WHISTLED over Bolan's head, and he responded with a short burst from his M-16 A-1, the 5.56 mm tumblers chewing wood and plaster, driving one of Liu's commandos back and under cover. Rather than move on and leave an enemy behind him, risking a bullet in the back, the Executioner unclipped a frag grenade, armed the bomb and lobbed it overhand into the pantry where the gunner had concealed himself. He kept on moving, put another wall and twenty feet between himself and the explosion when it came.

The shrilling smoke alarms were almost loud enough to mask the sounds of small-arms fire ahead, reminding Bolan of the sound effects from countless sci-fi movies, where the spaceship is about to self-destruct. He kept on going, tried to shut the noise from his mind, aware that shooting at the far end of the corridor could only mean Brad Phillips had engaged the enemy.

The lights winked out, and Bolan cursed the sudden darkness. It made little difference whether someone on the other side had thrown a master switch, or fire and shrapnel had destroyed sufficient wiring to cut off the flow of power.

Either way, he would be fighting in the dark from that point on.

Or, maybe not.

He reached into his fanny pack and withdrew a compact pair of goggles, pausing long enough to slip them on. The goggles made a high-pitched whining noise as Bolan pressed a button on the left, and then the hallway was illuminated for him in a washed-out greenish color. It wasn't the best device for reading small-print novels in a basement after lights-out, but it gave him all the edge he needed over Vincent Liu and company.

The sound of shots had sputtered out in front of him, and while he still heard voices calling from the dark behind him, others from the grounds outside, he was advancing on what seemed to be a dead zone in the house. No sooner had he registered the sudden stillness, than he saw two bodies stretched out on the floor in front of him.

One had collapsed against the wall, to Bolan's left; the other was a twisted sprawl of arms and legs, a few yards farther on. He checked the nearest of the bodies first, a young Chinese, not dead, but fading fast with three or four wounds in the chest. His stomach knotted as he moved to stand above the second body, looking worse than death in the unearthly greenish light imparted by his goggles.

Phillips.

Bolan knelt beside the Mountie, felt in vain for any vestige of a pulse. He had been hit repeatedly. The navy turtleneck he wore was soaked through with blood, and one round had entered below his jawline on the right. With any luck at all, he had been dead before he hit the floor.

He doubled back, picked up the Chinese gunner's pistol, sniffing at the muzzle. It hadn't been fired, which told him someone else had to be responsible for Phillips's death. The recent sounds of gunfire told him *when* the man had died, but it didn't identify his killer. Bolan knew the gunman hadn't doubled back along the corridor, or else they would have met.

Which meant that he was still somewhere ahead.

He picked up the Uzi and looped its sling across one shoulder. He left Brad Phillips where he lay. The enemy could do him no more harm, and packing Phillips out would mean he had to scrub his mission before he dealt with Vincent Liu.

The double doors stood open on a pillared porch that could have graced a planter's mansion in the antebellum South. *Gone With the Wind,* and then some. So it would be for the Triad in Vancouver, if he got a good, clean shot at Vincent Liu.

There was a fifty-fifty chance that he had missed the red pole, passed him somewhere in the smoky darkness of the house, and Bolan knew that he would have to check it out unless his hunch paid off. If Liu was still in front of him, attempting to evacuate the premises and let his soldiers face the music on their own, then the Executioner should expect to see him any moment—climbing into a Mercedes-Benz, for instance, just as Bolan reached the porch.

He heard the engine come to life, gears shifting smoothly, then the vehicle was rolling, almost locking bumpers with a BMW as speed took priority over safe driving.

Bolan didn't have a chance to think about what happened next. He snapped the rifle to his shoulder, left hand braced against the fat drum magazine, his finger curled around the M-203's trigger as he lobbed a high-explosive round from fifty feet away. The Benz was built for safety, but it wasn't armor-plated, an extravagance that Liu had never needed in the past. The HE round exploded as it struck the vehicle's left-rear fender, ripping through the trunk as if a giant can opener was at work, the left-rear tire reduced to flapping tatters on its rim.

Liu lost control, smoke trailing behind his car as it began to swerve in the direction of a decorative hedge that the outline of the driveway. He had speed enough to breach the hedge, but not to drive completely through it. The vehicle got hung up on stubborn juniper, the engine stalling out.

Bolan reloaded as he cleared the steps, another HE round in case he had to finish off the Benz that way, but Liu wasn't prepared to sit and wait for death. He had already scrambled from the car when the soldier got there, racing for the cover of the trees. His legs were fighting him, still shaky from the blast that wrecked his getaway and trashed the car, but he was making it, would probably have found a place to hide if Bolan had been any slower off the mark.

A burst of 5.56 mm slugs reached out to bring him down. The red pole jerked and stumbled, threw one arm out in a hopeless bid to catch himself and went down on his face. He recovered from the fall in nothing flat and struggled up on hands and knees. He wobbled, turning back toward Bolan, but he kept a firm grip on the pistol in his hand.

The gun he used to kill Brad Phillips.

Bolan used the M-203 launcher one more time. It was excessive, swatting flies with a sledgehammer, but he didn't mind. His afternoon withdrawal from Liu's bank would cover the expenses for matériel, and then some.

The explosion seemed to vaporize his target in a heartbeat. It was an illusion, smoke and flying sod concealing Liu, but the reality was close enough. Liu's mother would have had a hard time recognizing him, and Bolan didn't have to check the red pole's pulse to see if he was dead.

Behind him, from the general direction of the house, he heard more soldiers shouting, getting organized for a pursuit into the darkened woods. A wailing siren, followed instantly by others, seemed to change their minds, though, and he had the darkness to himself as he retreated from the mansion, jogging back in the direction of his rental car.

It might go hard on Phillips in the press, at first, but Bolan had a hunch that Hal Brognola would be able to suggest another angle for reporters working on the story. By the time the big Fed finished, Phillips could wind up a martyr, one more blameless victim of the Triads in Vancouver. Maybe he would even get a posthumous citation, when the brass had time to think it through.

As for the other questions that would go unanswered, Bolan didn't know or care how journalists would speculate about the death of Vincent Liu. Strategic leaks from Stony Man and the RCMP could light a fuse under the Triads, maybe drop some hints of their involvement with the Chinese Communists that would spread ripples all the way across the vast Pacific.

As for Luk Pang, he had been fortunate so far, but it couldn't go on forever. Bolan had a fair idea where Pang was going, and he could get confirmation from the Farm.

He felt another late-night journey coming on, and Death would be there waiting for him, at the other end.

9

New York City

It was a brand-new day in Chinatown, but Luk Pang was still caught up in the recurring nightmare that had dogged him for the past two days. He had slept briefly, with the aid of alcohol and pills, to wake up feeling groggy, vaguely nauseated, like a beaten man. The pale light streaming through his window hurt his eyes.

The spacious fifth-floor apartment belonged to Phillip Soo, Pang's driver. It was situated on the southwest corner of the intersection formed by Pell and Doyers streets. A century before, when brutal Tong wars were the rule in Chinatown, that intersection had been nicknamed Bloody Corner in the local newspapers, a tribute to the many victims killed by pistol shots or hatchet blows. Today, the tenants of that one-time killing ground were more concerned with round-eyed tourists than they were with debts of honor paid in blood.

This morning, Luk Pang knew that much of the uneasiness he felt had more to do with what was coming than the bloodshed that had gone before. He had postponed communication with the Dragon much too long already. There was bound to be some criticism of his failure to report before he left Vancouver, and while Pang was fairly confident that he could sell a passable excuse, the Dragon's memory was long. He kept a mental list of errors and infractions, easily recalled when he was dealing with particular subordinates. Too many errors—sometimes only one, if it was serious enough—and there was bound to be some consequence. Pang thought of men he knew who had been maimed or murdered, others who had simply disappeared, and hoped that he wasn't about to join them. Prayer was beyond him, as a lifelong Communist, but Luk Pang did the next best thing: he kept his fingers crossed.

The late reports from Canada were grim enough. He knew that Vincent Liu was dead, and CNN reported that a white man's body had been found among Liu's soldiers in the smoking ruin of his home. The round-eye's name had been withheld, until his next of kin was notified, but there were rumors on the street—and on the airwaves—that he wore a badge.

What did it mean?

It was another riddle Pang would have to deal with, to try to puzzle out what had become of the well-ordered world he knew, where he received commands directly from the Dragon, passed them on to his subordinates and saw his every wish fulfilled without an argument. Luk Pang felt like a man who awakened from a coma to discover that his job, his family and all his friends had been wiped out by some catastrophe, compelling him to start afresh with nothing, broken, destitute.

The truth wasn't that grim, of course. New York was still secure, and he could always blame the 14K for the attacks out west. It could be true, for all Pang knew. The Triads thrived on internecine warfare, sabotage, intrigue. Pang sometimes felt the leaders saw their lives as incomplete if they weren't conspiring to assassinate one another, craving blood for some imaginary insult dating back a quarter century or more. Fantastic profits from the drug trade kept them agitated, each one looking for a way to screw the rest and thereby keep a larger fortune for himself.

It was an angle, anyway, and if Luk Pang wasn't convinced, perhaps he could persuade the Dragon that he was.
A little time was all he needed, breathing room in which to
learn the name and number of his enemies. That done,
elimination would be relatively simple. All he had to do was
tell the 14K who had been knocking off their bright young
men, and they would do the rest.

But first Pang had to make that call.

He checked his watch, did simple math and knew it would
be shortly after dusk in Hong Kong. *Tomorrow's* dusk, that
was, thanks to the date line. How marvelous it would have
been to step inside a time machine, check out the future to
prevent his enemies from making their next move or turn the
clock back to destroy them two days earlier, before the San
Francisco raids.

Too late.

Luk Pang would work with what he had and make the
best of it.

But first he had to tell the Dragon he had failed. Again.

NEW YORK HAD BEEN the only real choice, after Hong
Kong, and it didn't take the Stony Man computers long to
verify that Luk Pang was back in the United States. In fact,
his movements had been followed—loosely, it was true, but
followed all the same—by a variety of local, state and federal law-enforcement agencies since he had first set foot in
North America. The FBI and DEA, NYPD Narcotics and
the Nassau County D.A.'s office had been watching Pang at
home, while Interpol agents of the CIA contributed their
input on his links to the administration in Beijing. Unfortunately Luk Pang wasn't a diplomat who could be sent
home on suspicion of illegal acts, nor had the marathon
surveillance produced any single piece of evidence that
would support a criminal indictment leading to imprison-
ment or deportation. Pang's repeated "social" contacts with
suspected Triad gangsters were on file, of course, but no one

had succeeded, yet, in eavesdropping on those protected conversations, finding out exactly what Pang's link to men like Sammy Ng and Vincent Liu might be.

In New York City, Pang's connection to the 14K was William Ma, a second-generation immigrant whose parents came to New York City in the midst of China's revolution. They were well connected at the time—Ma's father was a wealthy merchant with and supporter of the Kuomintang, with good friends in the D.C. China lobby—and a number of those personal connections had endured, while new ones were created over time. Few businessmen gained any prominence in pre-Communist China without accommodating the Triads, and Ma's father had gone a step further, taking the blood oath of membership himself. It became a family tradition when William was old enough to sign on, and he had risen through the ranks like a champion, assisted by a reputation that was equal parts ferocity and cunning.

Ma currently ran a chain of restaurants that spread from Chinatown through the five boroughs, but his major source of income in the past two decades had been heroin. His nickname in the 14K—"White Powder" Ma—was a fraternal tribute to his skill as an importer and distributor of China white. His customers included addicts in New York, Connecticut, New Jersey and the eastern half of Pennsylvania, few of whom had ever heard his name.

William Ma was a red pole in the grand Triad tradition, known among his fellows as a stone-cold killer, never prosecuted for the incidents that nailed his reputation down in Chinatown. His public face—as businessman, philanthropist and patron of the arts, a fixer who could serve up Chinese-bloc votes for a worthy cause or, off the record, for a price—had earned him write-ups in the *New York Times*, *New Yorker* magazine and *Forbes*. The articles contained no speculation on Ma's underworld connections or his role in flooding the East Coast with Asian heroin.

It was believed, by those who knew him well, that William Ma was physically and legally untouchable in Chinatown, a man who took the time to cover his tracks and took care of any problems in the embryonic stage, before they could result in major damage to his empire. And, until today, that view had been correct.

Mack Bolan wasn't bound by the rules that handcuffed the authorities, however. He didn't require search warrants or eyewitness testimony to make his case. He supplied his own probable cause.

White Powder Ma, for all his covert wars, had never faced an adversary quite like Bolan, one who couldn't be intimidated, bribed, persuaded or coerced.

He could be killed, of course, but stronger men than William Ma had tried and failed in that pursuit. Whole governments, in fact, had failed to bring him down.

In that respect, the Executioner and his intended target were alike, but the resemblance ended there. One killed for profit, to maintain his personal position in a predatory brotherhood of thieves and murderers; the other preyed on predators themselves. Ma's life had been devoted to pursuit of money, power and influence, while Bolan's was an endless quest for justice.

They were locked on a collision course, and while White Powder Ma was probably aware of the events out west, perhaps forewarned of danger in the wind by Luk Pang, he had no way of understanding the full gravity of his impending situation.

Macau

THE DRAGON FROWNED as he replaced the telephone receiver in its cradle, switched off the scrambler and leaned back in his swivel chair. He spent a contemplative moment staring at the ceiling, finally lit a British Player's cigarette and drew the smoke deep into his lungs.

The news from North America wasn't encouraging. Another man might have regarded it as a disaster, cause for mourning, but extreme emotion was as alien to Cheung Kuo as blond hair and blue eyes. If forced to go against his life-long training and adopt religious principles, he would have worshiped self-control.

The loss of Sammy Ng and Vincent Liu was inconvenient, to be sure, but men could always be replaced. The harsh glare of publicity surrounding their demise was worse, but that would pass in time, as new atrocities and fresh scandals came along to occupy the tiny minds of men and women weaned on tabloid journalism. Regional investigations of the 14K in San Francisco and Vancouver would disrupt his program for a while, but they should cause no lasting damage if the principals were wise enough to keep their wits about them, shut their mouths and weather out the storm.

His primary concern, this night, lay in the riddle of the man or men responsible for the attacks. Luk Pang had nothing to contribute on that score, beyond a rumor that the round-eye executed in Vancouver had been some kind of policeman. That was extraordinary in itself, if true, since North American police primarily confined their vigilante impulses to beating blacks, Hispanics, Indians and "poor white trash." Cheung Kuo couldn't recall a case in living memory where officers had strayed so far outside the law to punish organized offenders. It was normally the other way around, with no end to cops who had their hands out, waiting for another bribe so they could look the other way, ignore narcotics traffic, prostitution, gambling—anything at all, in fact, that puritanical society denied its citizens by law.

The rumor's accuracy would be simple to check out, but even if the dead man was a cop, it still wouldn't suggest that any agency supported his activities. He might turn out to be a renegade or madman, even someone Vincent Liu had dealt with—maybe cheated—in the past.

Cheung Kuo didn't enjoy considering the other possibility, namely, that some intelligence agency or law-enforcement group not only knew what he was up to with the 14K, but had decided to oppose him by direct, subversive action. It wasn't what he expected from policemen in the West, and it would complicate his plans no end. Not ruin them, perhaps, but still...

He would delay informing Beijing of the temporary setback. There was no need to alarm the old men with a problem that would soon resolve itself. Few operations ran without a hitch, and Cheung Kuo's merger with the Triads had been paying handsome dividends for three years now. It was unfortunate that they had hit a snag—and quite a bloody one, at that—but he would ride it out, use every means at his disposal to correct the problem and return their vehicle of conquest to a steady course.

Recalling Luk Pang would be a start, but when the Dragon thought about it, he decided it would cause more problems than it solved. Pang had established close connections with the Chinese underworld in Canada and the United States. He had their trust, at least to some degree, and had established a rapport. No doubt, an order from the leaders of the 14K in Hong Kong would convince the scattered red poles to cooperate with Pang's successor, but it seemed to Kuo that a new disruption, coming at a time when so much had already gone awry, would only make things worse.

Pang would get another chance—one *last* chance—to discover what was happening in North America and put it right. Above all else, the virus could not be allowed to spread beyond the States, where violence was a daily fact of life in any case. The U.S.A. was critically important to their plan, but it wasn't the most important part right now. Their drugs, illegal aliens and other contraband were shipped from Southeast Asia, through the Philippines to Europe, Mexico, the States and Canada. Disruption of the pipeline closer to its source would be a greater problem than upheavals in the marketplace, no matter who got killed in San Francisco or Vancouver.

And New York was safe.

So far.

If anything should happen to their network in the city round-eyes called the Big Apple, Luk Pang would have to suffer for his negligence. Kuo had made it clear to his subordinate that any further losses would be unacceptable. If Pang couldn't control his territory, he would be removed—and when the Dragon spoke those words, it carried more weight than a simple threat of reassignment to another post. Removal, in the world they occupied, was normally a permanent condition.

Kuo hoped it wouldn't come to that, but if it did, the Dragon's appetite could easily accommodate his second-in-command.

New York City

BOLAN CHOSE the Fu-xie Fang-jian to launch his war in New York's Chinatown because of its location—near the district's heart, on Bayard Street—and equally because it was the property of William Ma. A stylish nightclub where the more affluent businessmen of Chinatown could brainstorm with one another, maybe treat a wealthy round-eye if they felt the urge, Fu-xie Fang-jian was justly famous for its chef, its wine cellar and its lovely hostesses, who were reportedly dismissed as being "too old" for the job when they turned twenty-five. It was the kind of story, spread by word of mouth, that would have had Caucasian feminists lined up to sue the club, but this was Chinatown, and no one with an ounce of sense hung any writs on William Ma.

The club opened its doors at 5:00 p.m. and served big-spending customers until the statutory closing time of 3:00 a.m. Beyond that, if selected favorites were ushered to a private room upstairs, where they could drink a little more and get to know the hostesses more intimately... well, whose business was it, anyway? Vice officers and legmen for the state liquor board were happy to turn a blind eye, in return for the payoffs and favors William Ma provided to his friends.

Mack Bolan, on the other hand, wasn't for sale.

A charter flight with special clearance from Vancouver had delivered Bolan to McChord Air Force Base, outside Tacoma, Washington, and he was flown directly from there to Beacon Hill, a U.S. Navy ammunition depot in New Jersey, ten miles from Manhattan as the buzzard flew. A clean civilian car was waiting for him there, and he was on the road before the brass at Beacon Hill had time to wonder who he was, or why their airstrip had been requisitioned for some sort of clandestine op. By 1:30 p.m., the Executioner was in Manhattan, on his way to Chinatown and an appointment with White Powder Ma.

He drove past Fu-xie Fang-jian in his Mazda MX3 and lucked into a parking spot a half block east. The day was clear but cool, and no one gave his knee-length overcoat a second glance. There were enough white tourists on the street that Bolan didn't stand out as the only round-eye in the neighborhood, and assorted shops and restaurants on Bayard Street were used to dealing with suppliers drawn from every color of the human rainbow.

The alley that Bolan took west from Bayard to the back door of the Fu-xie Fang-jian was relatively clean, no rats or human derelicts in evidence. Before he reached the far end and came out behind the club, he had already double-checked the Uzi slung beneath his arm and loosened the Beretta 93-R slightly in its holster. Whatever happened in the next few moments, Bolan was as well prepared as he would ever be.

The club was closed, and the soldier didn't have a clue if there would be employees on the premises, preparing for another night of high-priced revelry. He had no quarrel with dishwashers and janitors, but anyone who tried to interrupt his plans for taking out Ma's club would quickly come to grief.

The service door in back was locked, but Bolan used his picks and beat the lock in forty seconds flat. Inside, he listened carefully for any sounds of conversation or activity and came up empty. Still, he didn't let himself relax as he explored the club, the Uzi submachine gun in his hand ready to cut loose if he was challenged.

There was no one in the dining room, the separate cocktail lounge, the kitchen or the storeroom. Bolan was about to quit his search and get down to business, when he heard the faint, staccato click-clack sound of a computer keyboard emanating from behind a door marked Private, at the southeast corner of the club. It had to be the office, and he didn't bother knocking as he barged inside.

The man behind the desk was middle-aged, Chinese and dumbstruck by the vision of a white man with an automatic weapon standing on the threshold of his inner sanctum. Blinking rapidly behind his horn-rimmed spectacles, he seemed to weigh the odds of dying if he took some desperate action, finally deciding that it wasn't worth the risk.

"Are you the manager?"

"I am." There was a tremor in the high-pitched voice.

"You have a safe." No question, this time. It was safe to bet the odds.

The nightclub's manager didn't respond at once, considering his options, the futility of physical resistance, but his eyes flicked toward the wall on Bolan's left. A watercolor landscape was the only decoration on the wall, and Bolan quickly saw that it was hinged instead of hung, to hide a square, flush-mounted wall safe.

"Open it."

The man did as he was told, and Bolan smiled at the fat stacks of currency inside. He didn't need the money, but in dealing with the likes of William Ma, he liked to add insult to injury whenever possible.

"I'll need a bag or briefcase," Bolan told the manager.

"This is a bad idea," his captive said.

"I'll take my chances. Get the bag."

A moment later, when the money had been packed inside a gray attaché case, Bolan told the manager, "You're free to go now. Find yourself a telephone and call White Powder Ma. Tell him his club is out of business."

"What?" The older man couldn't believe his ears.

"If he has any questions, I'll get back in touch."

"I don't—"

The Uzi silenced him, its muzzle coming up beneath his chin. "No time for small talk," Bolan told him. "Hit the bricks."

He started in the office, dropping two or three of the incendiary sticks in every room, as he retreated to the service exit and the outside world. The first sharp tang of smoke was in his nostrils as he reached the alley and started back toward Bayard, toward his waiting car.

It was a start, but nothing more. He meant to stay in touch with William Ma from that point on, until he felt the time was right for him to nail the red pole and his Communist associate—together, if he got the chance, but separately, if nothing else would do.

Luk Pang wouldn't escape this time, if there was any way on earth to stop him. He had been fortunate in San Francisco and Vancouver, but his luck was running out.

MA WAS CURSING ROUNDLY in Cantonese as he slammed down the telephone. He felt the rush of angry color to his face, the throbbing ache behind his eyes that was the warning signal for a migraine coming on. He reached out with his fist and struck the telephone again, as if the silent plastic instrument were an extension of his nameless, faceless enemy.

He had been warned, knew all about the recent tragedies in San Francisco and Vancouver, but New York had always been a separate world from the West Coast. Ma had his own concerns, connections, friends and enemies. He had no reason to believe that anyone would follow Luk Pang across the continent and try to kill him here. It was illogical, almost insane.

But it was happening.

The rage came back, full force, and Ma suppressed an urge to pick up the offending telephone and fling it through the nearest window of his fifth-floor office to the street below. With his luck, he would probably be jailed for braining a pedestrian.

The firefighters had saved a portion of Fu-xie Fang-jian, but not enough to matter. It would be a write-off, for insurance purposes, unless the stingy bastards tried to claim that Ma had set the fire.

In fact, he knew it was a round-eye, a description from the frightened manager already circulating to his soldiers on the streets. He had provided the description to police, as well, for all the good that it would do. Ma didn't want the law to catch his enemy, since that would cheat him of his personal revenge.

He wanted justice—meaning blood—and that wouldn't be found in any white man's court of law.

Ma slapped the intercom and called for his lieutenants, staying behind his desk as they filed in. They didn't sit without permission, and it wasn't granted. Ma didn't intend to keep them long.

"We must—"

A loud *crack* from the window on his right cut off the red pole's words. He had begun to turn in that direction, thinking to himself that it had to be another pigeon blundering against the glass, when the skull of Richard Wu exploded like a melon with a cherry bomb inside. The gunner's blood and brains were everywhere, and then his body toppled over backward in boneless sprawl.

Before the distant echo of the shot was audible, another of the red pole's field commanders died before his eyes, the lower portion of his face disintegrating into crimson spray. The dead man staggered to his right, collided with the next in line and jarred his comrade far enough off-line that when the third round struck it was a chest shot, spouting blood from ruptured lungs.

"Sniper!"

Ma's shouted warning came too late for anyone but Danny Sing, and he was already in motion, breaking toward the exit, when a bullet slammed between his shoulder blades and drove his face into the nearest wall. Sing left a bloody smear to mark his passing as he slithered to the floor.

By that time, William Ma was underneath his desk and listening to bullets rake his office. One took out the telephone; another dropped a painting from the wall behind his desk; a third shattered the vase of fresh-cut flowers on his filing cabinet.

When it was over, and the chilling silence had returned, Ma took a moment to convince himself that it was safe to move. For all he knew, the sniper could be waiting for him, peering through a telescopic sight, prepared to fire again the moment Ma exposed himself. It was the shrill voice of his secretary, screaming from the open doorway, that convinced him he could stir without immediate reprisal from his unseen enemy.

He came out bellowing, a cornered lion more enraged by the embarrassment than any wound to flesh and bone he could have suffered in the shooting incident. He called for soldiers, guns, for vengeance. It was only when he saw his secretary gaping at him, dumbstruck, that Ma felt the liquid warmth, glanced down and realized that he had wet himself.

10

The thing you had to keep in mind while working China-town, Detective Sergeant Terry Sheppard told himself, was that the people you confronted would be different. It went beyond the superficial—their appearance, accent, dialects—and touched on something more profound, more fundamental. If you couldn't grasp that difference, then you might as well pack up and head back to the Bronx, leave Chinatown to someone who would understand.

In seven years with NYPD's crack Intelligence Division, Sheppard had been detailed to observe and document activities of Asian gangsters in the city. He was white, self-taught in Cantonese and had been working with a Chinese partner until last September, when a car wreck unrelated to the job had left him solo on the Triad beat. In time, there would probably be another Asian partner—for the sake of the department's image, if no other reason—but he had no beef with working solo in the meantime.

Tracking William Ma and his associates was frustrating, sometimes, but it had never been an occupation fraught with peril. Chinese mobsters—the established, older ones, at any rate—knew it was easier to buy a cop than kill one, safer in the long run to allow some snooping at the fringes of their empire, while the major cash and contraband was moved behind the scenes. If anyone had asked him, Terry Sheppard could have pointed Vice to several dozen whore-houses and gambling dens in Chinatown, or steered Narcotics to lofts where uncut China white was "stepped on," bagged and priced for distribution on the streets. If pressed, he could—reluctantly—have named a handful of detectives and a larger complement of uniformed patrolmen who were taking payoffs from the 14K. But he was working for Intelligence, which meant he was supposed to spy and eavesdrop, file reports that might or might not lead to action somewhere down the road.

Frustrating? Sure. Infuriating? Sometimes. Dull? Not once in five years working Chinatown.

This afternoon's excitement was the first real violence Sheppard had encountered in at least two years. The youth gangs were another story—here as anywhere they roamed the streets across America—but the explosive incidents in Chinatown that day were clearly aimed at William Ma and his machine. Someone was challenging the red pole, and that someone played for keeps.

The torch job at the Fu-xie Fang-jian was one thing, maybe an insurance job that Ma was blaming on a white man to divert suspicion from himself, but four men dead in Ma's own office was another story. Sniper fire, at that—the rarest kind of gangland killing, next to poison, you would ever see.

The Triads were no different than the Mafia, Hell's Angels or the Westies when it came to killing one another. Close-range shootings were the rule, a stabbing now and then, sometimes a bit of torture if the mark had made himself obnoxious to the brothers in some special way. Long-distance killing called for expertise few criminals possessed today, and it was also too remote to satisfy an angered gangster. Let the dirty bastard see death coming for him, watch him squirm before you pulled the trigger. Maybe have him beg on hands or knees, like there was any chance at all he would be spared.

More often, when the Triad saw a need to kill someone in Chinatown, the victim simply disappeared. If he was ever found—a circumstance unlikely in itself—the skeleton made it more difficult for medical examiners to state the cause of death, much less pin charges on specific executioners.

A public shooting, on the other hand, was meant to send a message. Someone had a challenge for the godfather of Chinatown, and he was pushing it, though it didn't have the feel of action sponsored by a rival Chinese gang.

The tall man stepped in front of Sheppard, holding up a laminated ID card, derailing Sheppard's train of thought. The ID marked him as an agent of the DEA, but there was something out of place. For one thing, he was too clean-cut.

"Detective Sheppard?"

"Sergeant. Right."

"Mike Blanski. You have a minute?"

"More or less."

"We need to talk," Bolan stated, glancing toward the shattered office windows overhead. "Not here, though."

"Oh?"

"It's sensitive."

"Okay," Sheppard said, curious. "Let's take a stroll."

THE FEAR WAS almost palpable to Luk Pang. He hated it, that helpless feeling, as he sat and waited for the noose to tighten, but his mind went blank when he began to cast about for viable alternatives.

And it was happening again, damn it, this time in New York.

Pang understood the difference between coincidence and a conspiracy. As a conspirator himself, he was adept at picking out the signs, reading between the lines. It was entirely possible, for instance, that a Triad soldier might be mugged and shot or struck and killed by a drunk driver in the middle of a gang war, and the incident would still be unrelated to the feud in progress. It was quite a different story, though, when three distinct and separate Triad families were attacked within as many days, each new aggression following the pattern of Pang's headlong flight across the continent.

Someone was tracking *him* and killing his associates among the 14K. That much had been apparent from the sniping of his personal lieutenants back in San Francisco, while police were still examining the prospects of a "Tong war." Round-eyes, possibly the same men, were involved in every case.

Pang hadn't shared the latter piece of news with William Ma, however. It was impossible to warn a red pole that he might soon be attacked, then see the prophecy come true, without accepting any of the blame. Ma was a clever thug, and he would draw his own conclusions. Pang would only strip himself of 14K support if he confessed his personal, unwitting role in the attacks. Unless he could present Ma with the names and whereabouts of his assailants, it would be a pointless sacrifice to put his own neck on the chopping block.

Two incidents in ninety minutes, and the wonder of it— based on what Luk Pang had seen was that the body count had stopped at four.

So far.

There would be more attacks, and there was nothing he could do to stop it. His most recent orders from the Dragon were specific: watch and wait. He wasn't to involve himself beyond the absolute necessities of self-defense. Let Ma protect his businesses as any other warlord should.

Pang meant to stay in touch, aware that Ma was now his last, best hope of living through the ordeal that had dogged him for the past two and a half days. Pang had a handful of associates—mostly illegals—operating out of New York's Chinatown, but few of them would pass for soldiers; the majority had never even held a gun, much less fired shots in anger at another human being.

Pang wasn't afraid to kill, but he didn't require a bullet in the brain to know he would be outmatched and outgunned in any contest with his present foe. Police or otherwise, these faceless men were skilled assassins, trained to kill, with plenty of experience behind them. Pang regarded it as weakness when they sometimes let a witness live, but even that could serve their plan by spreading rumors, fear and dread.

He felt that he should leave Philip Soo's apartment, go somewhere—anywhere—and find a better hiding place. His latest conversation with the Dragon left Pang with a bad taste in his mouth, a sneaking hunch that his superiors would try to blame him for the incidents in San Francisco, in Vancouver and, now, in New York. The Dragon clearly understood that Pang was one of the enemy's primary targets, and it would be more cost-efficient in the long run to eliminate one man than wage a long and costly war. The very secrecy of their assailants helped Pang out, in that regard. Without a name or something else to guide him on his way, the Dragon couldn't make an offer to the enemy. A human sacrifice, if such was planned, would be in vain.

Increasingly Pang thought it would be wise for him to find a hiding place, not only from his nameless enemies, but from his so-called friends, as well. Who could predict what shape the next assault would take, or where it would originate?

Pang thought of hiding out from William Ma, but then decided that his best defense against the red pole would be to cooperate with Ma in every way, make it apparent that he would do anything within his power to destroy the men who had them both marked for destruction. He could alleviate—if not eradicate—Ma's doubts, while keeping men and guns around him in a strong defensive ring.

It all made perfect sense.

He would alert Ma first, to let the red pole know that he was coming. Call him on the telephone immediately, if he could get through. Ma had his hands full at the moment, with police investigating the assassination of his four lieutenants and the Fu-xie Fang-jian fire. It might take time to reach him, longer yet to sell the notion of a live-in house-guest who was being stalked by one or more professional and highly competent assassins.

Pang thought he could pull it off if he was calm and per-suasive, provided he didn't raise Ma's hackles by adopting what the round-eyes called "an attitude." It was the wrong time to be pushing William Ma, but he could easily present the notion as a plan of mutual defense: Pang's quick wit and his international connections paired with Ma's raw nerve and private army. As a team, the two of them would be, if not invincible, at least considerably stronger than when standing separately. There was a chance Ma might resist, but he was still accountable to his superiors in Hong Kong, and those worthy gentlemen were very much beholden to the Dragon.

It wasn't a perfect plan, but Pang could think of nothing better at the moment. He retreated from the window to a low-slung coffee table, where five guns were laid out: three semiautomatic pistols, one sawed-off shotgun with a fold-ing metal stock and a mini-Uzi machine pistol. Spare mag-azines, together with a box of 12-gauge buckshot rounds, were situated in between the weapons.

They were ready for a siege, if it should come to that, but Pang preferred to take his chances somewhere else. Ma had made arrangements for the day when trouble found him, never quite believing it would happen, but he took precau-tions all the same.

It would require some sweet talk and persuasion, but Pang meant to take full advantage of his allies preparations. He wouldn't be left out in the cold this time, with no protection from the storm.

Survival was the top priority. Pang would consider the requirements of the People's Revolution later.

If he lived.

THEY STROLLED as far as Bolan's Mazda MX3, a block east of the shooting scene. With some misgivings, Terry Sheppard climbed into the shotgun seat as Bolan slid behind the wheel. When they had covered half a block in silence, Sheppard said, "You want to tell me who you really are?"

"I showed you my ID," Bolan replied.

"Right. Thing is, the DEA has rolling stock up the wazoo. They don't rent cars from Avis, last I heard."

It was as good a lead as any. Bolan frowned and said, "I'm not supposed to be in town."

"Oh, yeah? Why's that?"

"You've obviously had your eye on William Ma," Bolan said.

"So?"

"And you're watching his associates." He phrased it as a statement, not a question.

"Where appropriate," Sheppard replied, quoting from the book.

"Of course. So you're familiar with a Chinese gentleman named Luk Pang."

The name made Sheppard grimace. "Ah," he said. "The spook."

"You worked that out?"

"We've got a few connections," Sheppard told him, "even if it *is* New York. I plug into the Bureau's network, when I can, and I've got friends at Langley."

"That's a bonus."

"Every now and then. What's DEA's connection to Beijing?"

"I'm not with the DEA," Bolan said, wading in a little deeper as they motored east through Chinatown.

"So, you're confessing to a felony impersonation here? I should advise you of your rights before you get too talkative."

"I've heard it all before. You can save your breath."

"So what's the deal?"

"Pang and his people have some kind of merger cooking with the 14K. We don't have all the details yet, but China white is part of it, along with traffic in illegal immigrants and military hardware. They've been slick enough to hide their tracks so far, and we've got nothing that would stand in court."

"Sounds like an old familiar song," the sergeant said.

"We've put a new twist on the chorus," Bolan told him. "Something more aggressive than your standard sit-and-wait procedure."

"Oh?"

"How dedicated are you to the book?" Bolan asked, shifting gears.

"You mean, how dedicated am I to my pension?"

"If that's how it plays."

"I do my time, file my reports," the sergeant said.

"I've seen them," Bolan told him.

It was an exaggeration, granted, but he had received a briefing from the crew at Stony Man. There was a bright detective sergeant in Intelligence, they told him, who was maybe getting sick and tired of futile stakeouts, filing endless paperwork without results, a gung-ho kind of guy who had been held back by the brass. At least, they said, it couldn't hurt to check him out. If he decided to cooperate, the Executioner would find a mother lode of precious information at his fingertips.

"Let's cut to the chase," Sheppard said.

"Works for me," Bolan answered. "I look at you and see a cop who joined the force to do some good, take bad guys off the street and make this town a cleaner place."

"So what?"

"You bust your hump six days a week, God only knows the hours, building up all kinds of cases on the Triads here in Chinatown. Connections, contacts, trade routes, friends and enemies. You type it up in triplicate, and one of your superiors decides to stick it in a file he may or may not read some time next month, if he remembers, if he has the time. You start to wonder if he's stupid, just plain lazy or if someone from the 14K is sweetening his coffee on the side.''

''I'm not aware of any officers—''

''Does that include Banducci?'' Bolan interrupted him. ''Or Flynn?''

The names had come from one of Sheppard's confidential field reports, relayed by Aaron Kurtzman at the Farm, a pair of dirty aces tucked away in Bolan's sleeve.

''That's confidential information, damn it!'' Sheppard snapped.

''I wouldn't dream of sharing it. You want rotten apples on the job, that's your decision. We've got problems of our own in Washington, like dealing with Beijing in public while they sneak around and try to stab us in the back.''

''That's not my territory, friend.''

''The shit they're moving winds up on your streets,'' Bolan stated. ''Someone has to make a stand.''

''Which means?''

''I'm working on a special strike team,'' Bolan told him, knowing that the next few moments would make all the difference in the world. The next few moments would produce a brand-new ally, or an enemy who could expose him to the world.

''What kind of strike team?'' Sheppard asked suspiciously.

''Let's say we're more concerned with stopping Pang and shaking up the 14K than following the rules of evidence.''

He let it go at that, but Sheppard's mind was quick enough to make the obvious connections. Silent for another block, the sergeant's voice contained a mix of awe and outrage when he spoke again.

''I don't believe this shit!'' he said. ''*You* made the hit on Ma. That's what you're saying, isn't it?''

''I don't go in for confession.''

''Jesus Christ! Four people dead, back there.''

"Four Triad officers. How many do you think they've killed, with guns or China white?"

"That's not the way it works," Sheppard said.

"If it *worked*, Pang would have been arrested or deported years ago. If it worked, the Triads would have been wiped out before they got a foothold in the States. You know as well as I do how the system works."

"So, you just throw the rules away?"

"New game, new rules," Bolan said. "You don't ride to work on horseback, Sergeant. We don't fight with sticks and stones—or writs and warrants."

"Why tell me?"

"You have dirt on Chinatown we'd have to spend another decade digging up. By that time, it would be too late ... for everyone."

"You think I'd go along with this? Assassination? Terrorism?"

"No one's asking you to pull a trigger," Bolan said. "You work for the Intelligence Division. We need up-to-date intelligence."

"I don't believe this."

"You believe your own reports, though, right? You know what's going on in Chinatown these days, and what nobody's doing to prevent it."

Sheppard frowned and shook his head. "You've got my paperwork," he said. "I don't know how, but that's your business. Anyway, what more—"

"I never knew a cop who wrote down everything he knew. Some of it would sound insane on paper—how you spot a bad guy from a distance, by his walk, the way he lights his cigarette. Some of it, if you put it down on paper, would send half your cases up in smoke. I want the inside story. Things you've seen but didn't share. I need to know Pang and his buddies inside out."

"I could wind up in prison," Sheppard said.

"If you start feeling guilty and confess," the Executioner replied. "Your people won't get anything from me or mine."

"You say."

"That's right."

The sergeant turned away from him, stared out his window at the passing shops. "I'll have to think about it," he replied, at last.

"Sounds fair."

THE RAGE would come and go, but William Ma was wise enough to know he had to control it, channel it, or else it might destroy him. Angry men did stupid things and brought themselves to grief. Managing an empire on the wrong side of the law required a certain measure of intelligence, however primitive, and Ma wasn't the kind of man to let emotions rule his mind.

There would be time enough for wreaking havoc on his enemies when they had been identified, tracked down and isolated. Then, and only then, would he unleash his fury on the dogs who had humiliated him in public. In the meantime, though, he had to watch his back, take every possible precaution to protect himself.

And that meant reaching out to the police.

The man who sat across the desk from Ma was in his fifties, somewhat overweight, with iron gray hair receding from a freckled forehead. The aroma of his foul cigar reminded Ma of rubbish burning at the dump. His suit and topcoat almost matched the color of his hair.

The gray man was Lieutenant Arthur Brock, a ranking officer of NYPD's proud Intelligence Division, presently— and for the past eight years—assigned to Chinatown.

"You have no clues at all?" Ma let a bare hint of the anger and frustration he was feeling creep into his tone.

"Shell casings from the rooftop," Brock replied. "Winchester Magnums, if that tells you anything. We find the gun, my guess would be the lab can match ballistics—the extractor marks and firing pin, at least. Don't know about the bullets, till the M.E. gets done with your people.''

"Nothing else?''

"The guy's a marksman, obviously,'' Brock went on. "He didn't drop his driver's license at the scene or anything like that. There's maybe one chance in a million for a latent print to show up on the brass. I wouldn't hold my breath on that if I was you.''

"No one observed this marksman, going in or out? It was broad daylight, I believe.''

Brock smiled at that. "You're asking me? When was the last time any witnesses from Chinatown cooperated with the fuzz? Somebody got a peek at Davy Crockett, your boys have a better chance of hearing it than I do.''

"Still, you have informants.''

"Not for shit like this. You're thinking it's a white guy, am I right? My people are supposed to keep a watch on *you* and anyone you talk to, not some round-eyed tourist passing through.''

"I want your best men on the case.''

"Oh, really?''

"Why is that amusing?''

"Oh, maybe because my best man has a hard-on for your whole damned operation, Billy. You remember Terry Sheppard, don't you? Yeah, I thought so. I've been burying his paperwork on you for years.''

"He still takes orders,'' Ma insisted. "He will do what you command.''

"It's not his field of expertise, a thing like this. He likes to watch your cutting plants and nooky cribs.''

"I want the best,'' Ma repeated, with no room for argument.

Brock shrugged and spoke around his fat cigar. "Hey, suit yourself. I saw him on the street outside your office, as it was. I'll keep an eye on him and let you know if he gets anything."

"I cannot overstate how critical this is," Ma said.

"Hey, we don't need a gang war, any more than you do. Makes us look bad, if you get my drift."

"Then do your job, Lieutenant," the red pole told him, scowling. "Save us both, before it is too late."

11

The brothel on Mulberry Street was nothing special. Ten girls working in an old three-story walk-up, red brick fronting on the street, no sign that would identify the business as to type. The address was enough. Neither the locals nor potential customers required a red light flashing on the doorstep to remind them what was going on inside.

Surveillance was a problem in broad daylight. He could only dawdle past the other shops on Mulberry so long, before his window shopping got him noticed in unhealthy ways. The brothel would have sentries posted, even though he couldn't spot them from the street, and Bolan was a round-eye on his own in Chinatown, no wife and kiddies trailing in his wake to fit the usual Joe Tourist image.

Any move he planned to make, the Executioner knew he would have to make it soon. All things considered, he decided that the best thing he could try was the direct approach. See how it played if he was just another horny white man with an address he had picked up "from a friend."

The afternoon was getting on, and Bolan put a little stagger in his walk as he crossed Mulberry. Make that a tipsy, horny white guy, out to get his ashes hauled. He wouldn't pass the sniff test, but appearance had to count for something. All he needed was an edge, some way to get his foot inside the door.

His raincoat and the jacket underneath were both unbuttoned, playing to the sloppy-drunk disguise—and not so incidentally providing him with rapid access to the hidden arms he carried. In a pinch, he calculated he could bring the Uzi or the silencer-equipped Beretta into play within a fraction of a second.

Six steps up to reach the stoop, and Bolan pressed the small enamel button mounted close beside the plain red door. He counted forty seconds, was about to try again when someone turned the dead bolt, fumbled briefly with a second latch and eased the portal open.

Bolan found himself confronted by a Chinese gunner in his twenties, hardware bulging underneath his left arm, like a misplaced breast beneath his polyester sport coat. Smiling like an idiot, the Executioner stepped closer, placing one hand on the door and leaning into it.

"Where's all the girls?" he asked, enough slur in his words to simulate a buzz.

"We're closed," the doorman said.

"Don't give me that!" He put enough belligerence in his tone to sound convincing. "I know the score. You want the cash up front, it's not a problem."

He was on the threshold now, head down, his left hand fumbling in a trouser pocket. Getting pissed, the doorman placed a hand on Bolan's chest, prepared to push him backward, down the steps.

"I said we're closed!"

His arm was pinned before he knew it, painful pressure on the wrist and elbow. The Beretta's custom sound suppressor was plugged into the socket of his left eye, grinding just enough to make the shooter gasp.

"I heard you," Bolan said, no longer slurring. He took the young man's pistol, stuck it in his belt and shoved the angry gunner back a pace, just out of reach.

"Who are you?"

"Trouble," Bolan told him. "If you've got a way to roust the girls out all at once, you'd better use it."

"Why?"

"Because you're going out of business." Bolan pulled back his coat and jacket to reveal grenades clipped on his belt.

The gunner reached around behind him, found another button on the wall and mashed it with his thumb. A heartbeat later, soft, almost melodic chimes began to sound upstairs, accompanied by a stampede of running feet. The signal for a raid, Bolan guessed, just in case the vice squad ever ran amok by accident.

Nine women were crowded in the parlor when he got there, following the doorman. None of them was dressed in more than filmy lingerie, but modesty wasn't a problem here. They focused on the gun in Bolan's hand and didn't give a damn if he was checking out the goodies with a small, appreciative smile.

"It's time to go," he told them, noting blank expressions on approximately half the faces. Turning toward the shooter, he said, "Tell them."

Bolan's hostage spoke rapidly in Cantonese, and there was barely time for them to step aside before the young women started making tracks. They hit the sidewalk running, fled without a backward glance or an apparent thought to where they would find clothes or transportation.

"You, too," Bolan told the shooter, noting the young man's immediate relief as he took off.

The three grenades were thermite, guaranteed to burn down almost anything constructed by the hands of man. On detonation, they released a burst of white-hot coals that were designed to eat through tempered steel, concrete and human flesh with equal ease. It would take special chemicals to douse that fire, and Ma's brothel would be a total write-off by the time firefighters managed to control the blaze.

He pitched the first incendiary can upstairs, dropped off a second in the kitchen and left the last one in the parlor as he moved back toward the street. A few pedestrians were loitering around the stoop, most of them men, still staring after the half-naked girls, and while a few of them tracked Bolan with suspicious eyes, they made no move to intercept him. By the time smoke started pouring from the building, he was in his car and rolling south on Mulberry, toward the next mark on his hit list.

OPIUM DENS enjoyed their heyday in nineteenth-century America, before the first *Pure Food and Drug Act* started cleaning up the dangerous, chaotic trade in pharmaceuticals. Old-fashioned vices still had their adherents, though, and opium had never faded altogether from the drug scene, even in the face of economic challenges from morphine, heroin and rock cocaine. For many Chinese addicts, it was still the drug of choice, less costly than refined derivatives, for some a twisted kind of cultural connection to their homeland of antiquity.

The den in Chatham Square was situated in a basement, with a separate air conditioner to circulate the pungent atmosphere without alerting or alarming upstairs neighbors. One flight down, a naked bulb outside the door glared in any new arrival's face while he was scrutinized from inside, through a fish-eye lens.

By the time Bolan was ready to punch the buzzer, he had smashed the bulb and stepped to one side of the peephole, waiting for a shadow to betray the lookout's presence. When he saw it coming, Bolan's move was swift and sure. He snapped a kick that smashed the lock and punched the door half-open, braining the gunner coming to check out the new arrival. A buttstroke to the man's temple with the Beretta guaranteed that he'd stay down.

Bolan edged inside, the compact gas mask from his pocket giving him a bug's-eye view of his surroundings. Even with the mask on, he could sense a difference in the atmosphere, before he passed a second door and found himself inside the den. Cheap wooden bunks were stacked on either side of him, resembling the cabin layout at a poor boy's summer camp, perhaps the passenger compartment of a slave ship from another century.

Approximately half the bunks were occupied as Bolan moved along the narrow center aisle. An average night? He had no way of knowing, no real interest in the groggy smokers. Some of them were watching him with cloudy eyes, the rest oblivious to the intrusion, each man clinging to his pipe as if it were the only thing that mattered in the world.

For some, perhaps it was.

A scowling bouncer moved to block him, coming out of nowhere. Bolan wasted no time on negotiation, shooting the gunner in the face and stepping across his body, moving toward the rear, where the proprietor would have his office. The Executioner tried the knob before he kicked the door and found it unlocked.

A short, fat man was wedged behind an Army-surplus metal desk, conferring with a younger, thinner man who stood beside him. They were checking entries in a ledger, both men startled by the new arrival who had joined them uninvited.

Honor or a nervous disposition made the young man reach inside his jacket for a weapon. Bolan put a parabellum round between his eyes and slammed him backward, watching him sprawl facedown beside the desk.

"Your turn," he told the fat man, waiting.

"I'm unarmed." As soon as the words left his mouth, the Chinese made a move toward the top drawer of his desk.

The Beretta spit one 9 mm round, the fat man spinning in his chair on impact, slumping awkwardly, a slow glide to the dirty floor. He wound up in a heap beneath the desk, legs tangled, one arm thrown above his head like someone posing for a boudoir photograph.

He could have torched the office, dropped incendiaries in among the bunks, but toasting spaced-out junkies wasn't Bolan's style. Instead, he left the front door open when he left, paused long enough to punch the fire alarm next door as he was passing by.

Let someone with a badge and uniform sort out the mess, decide which questions William Ma's front men should answer when the smoke cleared. It wasn't much, in terms of inconvenience to the 14K, but Bolan left no slimy stone unturned.

Three blocks away, he found a public telephone, the booth disguised as a pagoda, slipped inside and tapped out the number for NYPD headquarters at One Police Plaza. When the operator answered, Bolan asked for Sergeant Terry Sheppard, in Intelligence. Thirty seconds later he was listening to a familiar voice.

"Sheppard."

"This is Blanski. You remember me?"

"Indeed I do."

"We need to talk."

"So talk."

"Not on the telephone."

The sergeant hesitated, thinking that one over. Finally he said, "Okay. You still in Chinatown?"

"I'm mobile," Bolan said.

"How long's it been since you checked out the top of the Empire State Building?"

"A while."

"See you there in forty minutes."

HE HAD TO BE CRAZY, Sheppard thought, as he stood waiting for the elevator doors to close. Five other people were in the car, plus the attendant in his uniform, and it still felt like something from the *Twilight Zone*.

He had a rendezvous with some guy who was maybe DEA, most likely not, to talk about a half-baked move against the 14K. If Sheppard had been thinking straight, he told himself, he would have gone to his superiors at once, the minute Blanski spelled out his crazy program. He would be on the right side of the problem now, instead of waiting to hear more preposterous ideas from someone who was already as good as dead.

Or, maybe not.

The mix was heating up in Chinatown, with two more strikes since he had spoken to the "maybe" Fed. That didn't mean that Blanski was responsible, of course, but if he was, what, then?

Once the tallest building in the world, the Empire State now ranked after the World Trade Center and the Sears Roebuck Building in Chicago. Even so, the glass-walled upper observatory, some 1,250 feet above street level, was plenty high enough for Sheppard, offering a panoramic view for fifty miles in all directions when the air was clear. Today, a smoggy haze had cut that visibility by half, but Sheppard didn't mind. He had eyes only for the tall man who was waiting for him, at the window facing eastward, when he left the elevator car.

"You're early," Sheppard said, as he came up on Bolan's left.

"I made good time."

"And you've been busy, too."

"A bit."

"So, this is how it goes, eh? No more warrants, no more trials?"

"Not this time. Think of it as martial law in miniature."

"I must have missed that class at the police academy."

"It's something new," Bolan said with a crooked smile.

"And you're expecting me to join, like it was just another drive around the park."

"I'm not expecting anything. We could use your help, but we're not drafting anyone."

"When you say *we* . . ."

"Then I've said all I can. You want to drop a coin, the buck stops here, with me."

"What would I say?"

"You'd think of something," Bolan assured him. "I hope it doesn't come to that."

"It hasn't, yet."

"Still thinking?"

Sheppard hesitated. "No," he said at last. "I guess my mind's made up."

"So, which way did it go?"

"I'm here," the sergeant said. "What is it that you need?"

"I want to put the touch on Luk Pang. We lost him, coming into New York City. Can you give me some idea of where he's hiding out?"

"Not off the top," Sheppard said, "but I have my sources. I can ask around."

"Okay. That ought to sew it up."

"And when you get the address, then what?"

Bolan shrugged. "Maybe I'll pay a social call."

"Was that your calling card we found at Ma's office?"

"Does it matter?"

"I suppose it should," the sergeant said, "but I've been wondering about that very thing myself for quite awhile. You try to shovel shit uphill for six or seven years, it gets a little old."

"You're tired of shoveling?"

"Let's say that just for once I'd like to start on level ground."

"Seems fair."

"How do I get in touch?" Sheppard asked.

"Not a problem. I'll call you."

"All right. The way it looks right now, I should be working late around the office."

"Right."

Bolan stuck out a hand, and Sheppard grasped it. When their eyes locked, something passed between them. Understanding, for a start, and something else.

"I'd better split," he said at last, then turned and walked back to the elevator, wondering if he would ever see this man again.

NOW, WHO THE HELL was this guy?

Arthur Brock scowled as he asked himself the silent question, but no one noticed in the crowd of tourists wandering around the observation deck. So far, so good, but he was taking one hellacious chance. If Sheppard spotted him, Brock couldn't just pull rank; he knew that he would have to lay some kind of story out to make his presence something other than a weird and unbelievable coincidence.

He could always say that he was meeting an informant, but how would that look, a sergeant and lieutenant from Intelligence both having meets on the upper deck of the Empire State Building at the exact same time? It was ridiculous, a billion-to-one shot that no one would swallow, much less a veteran officer with Sheppard's smarts.

So, how about saying that he was following Sheppard to find out who he was talking to these days? It had the virtue of truthfulness, but where would that leave him? If he thought Sheppard was dirty, had his hand out like so many other guys in the department, there were mechanisms for entrapping him and taking care of business. A lieutenant didn't trail his men around the streets and spy on them himself. It simply wasn't done.

Best thing, in this case, was to keep his head down and avoid a confrontation. He headed back toward the elevator.

The long ride down gave Brock a chance to put his jumbled thoughts in order. There was Terry Sheppard on the observation deck, with some guy Brock had never seen before. It didn't prove a thing, but Sheppard *had* bailed out brief moments after he received a phone call at the office, and he *was* assigned full-time to Chinatown, specifically to William Ma and Luk Pang.

The man bending Sheppard's ear upstairs wasn't Chinese. That much was obvious to Brock, but it did nothing to relieve his troubled mind. The shooter, who had already left several living witnesses in Chinatown, wasn't an Asian, either. As it happened, his description could have fit the guy with Sheppard. If you made allowances for shock and fear, the tendency of witnesses to throw some bullshit in for flavor, hell, the two guys could be twins.

What kind of sense did that make? Sheppard was a good, straight-arrow cop, by all accounts. Too straight for some, in fact, since he would never take a handout when he did his turn with Vice. Of course, he never ratted out his brother officers, but the refusal to participate in an established system of corruption made him suspect, in and of itself. The transfer to Intelligence had been by mutual consent of Sheppard and his watch commander, moving Sheppard into a division where his taste for spying and surveillance served him well, and there was less temptation on the job.

Except in Chinatown.

Intelligence worked everything from terrorism, and sabotage to cults and wacky right-wing groups who thought there was a race war coming in America. The unit spent its time collecting information, snapping candid photographs, eavesdropping, infiltrating splinter groups the public never heard of or imagined: pedophiles with a religious twist; a tiny group in Queens who hated NASA and believed the several moon walks had been filmed in Hollywood, or maybe somewhere in Nevada; satanists who dabbled in pornography and drugs; new-agers with a taste for automatic weapons; Gay-bashing Nazis and militant lesbians.

The Triads were a part of it, for their political connections to the mainland, Hong Kong, Macau, Taiwan, the Philippines. Domestic crimes were parceled out to other units—Vice, Narcotics, Organized Crime—but the political angle belonged to Intelligence. Of course, it was inevitable that detectives watching William Ma to see if he played footsie with the Communists or smuggled aliens into the States would also pick up information on his other operations. Terry Sheppard did his paperwork and never made a stink when the reports disappeared into limbo, with no apparent action taken on his various recommendations. From all appearances, he was a team player. And yet . . .

Brock didn't think it was his own imagination playing tricks on him in recent days, when he caught Sheppard frowning over this or that command decision. Never grousing, mind you, but he didn't like the way Brock handled things—or *didn't* handle them, depending on your point of view. It was a long stretch, even so, to cast him as some kind of vigilante renegade, but still . . .

Brock had the lobby covered when his man came out, watched Sheppard leave the elevator, cross the lobby, step outside and disappear. There was no point in trailing him, and too much risk involved if Brock was spotted. At the moment, the lieutenant was more concerned about the other guy, determined to find out exactly who he was, what he was doing in New York and whether it had any link at all to William Ma or Chinatown.

If he could trace the men responsible for Ma's recent misfortune, Brock could make himself a killing, maybe salt away enough to make early retirement more attractive. Twenty, even thirty thousand dollars shouldn't be too much to ask, for the salvation of an empire.

Three long minutes later, Mr. X was stepping from the elevator, moving toward the street. Brock fell in step behind him, kept it casual, the way they taught him in surveillance school.

His subject had a rented Mazda in a city parking lot, two blocks away. Brock flagged down a taxi and badged the driver, handing him a twenty-dollar bill to get them started off on the right foot. They waited and saw the Mazda MX3 pull into traffic. The lieutenant spoke those magic words that only one cop in a thousand ever has the chance to say in any real-life situation.

"Follow that car."

IT DIDN'T HELP to brood on Terry Sheppard. He would either track down the necessary information and pass it on, or he wouldn't. In either case, the campaign would proceed. If necessary, Bolan would go door-to-door in Chinatown until he flushed his targets.

Meanwhile, he had at least a dozen targets waiting for him in the Chinese quarter, each and every one of which put money in the bank for William Ma. The loss of any one would sting; with luck he could take down five or six.

The porno studio was situated in a loft off Pell Street, near the Bowery. The building had no elevator, but he liked the stairs in any case. There was less chance of being ambushed at his destination if he wasn't riding in a six-by-six-foot metal coffin.

Bolan wasted no time jawing with the hardman on the door, letting the silenced Uzi do his talking from a range of twenty feet. The punk was grabbing for a pistol underneath his jacket, but he never had a chance to reach it, sprawling backward as the parabellum shockers opened up his chest.

The door was easy—three more rounds to smash the lock—and Bolan found himself inside the cheesy "soundstage." Mounted lights were shining on a queen-size bed, where two young Chinese girls were passing puberty the hard way, with a hairy-chested ape who looked like something outlaw bikers had rejected as beneath their standards. The director was a middle-aged Chinese; his crew was capturing the scene on 35 mm film and video, to serve both markets in an age that catered to diversity.

A burst from Bolan's Uzi took out the movie camera, film bursting from the canister. The cameraman went sprawling, one hand raised to stanch the flow of blood that sprang from where a bullet clipped his ear. Meanwhile, the video technician had already dropped his steady-cam and was retreating toward a neutral corner, hands raised high above his head.

"That's a wrap," Bolan said, pinning the director with a glare. "You work for William Ma?"

The man pretended not to understand, until the Uzi's still-warm muzzle kissed his forehead, then he started nodding like a puppet, babbling something about the years he spent in film school, waiting for his first big break, the whole nine yards. Ma had recognized his talent; it was just a part-time thing; the young women had been well paid and loved their work.

"You're fired," Bolan growled, swinging the Uzi in an arc and smashing it against the director's skull.

"The rest of you should hit the bricks," the Executioner advised them, already retreating toward the door. "Consider this your first and last review."

He guessed that it would be ten minutes, give or take, before the word got back to William Ma. In Chinatown, the grapevine was a swifter method of communication than the U.S. mail, and vastly more reliable.

In ancient China, prisoners condemned to die were most afraid of being sentenced to the "death of a thousand cuts," which bled a man or woman, leaving the person to writhe in pain for hours or days, instead of bringing sweet relief with one swing of the headsman's sword. Now it was Ma's turn to receive the venerable treatment, to sit and watch his empire bleed out through a string of flesh wounds, while he ran around and tried to make some sense of what was happening.

12

It was the hardest phone call Arthur Brock would ever make, the kind that made you grimace when you saw your own reflection in the bathroom mirror. Shame was part of it, along with the conditioned reflex that you never, ever ratted out a brother cop, no matter what he did.

But this was different, damn it! First of all, he wasn't ratting Terry Sheppard out to the headhunters from Internal Affairs, much less to the jackals of the press. Nothing he told William Ma would cast a shadow over the department. Hell, when the smoke cleared, NYPD just might have another hero martyr on its hands, the kind of name you threw around to boost appropriations at election time.

Looked at that way, he was doing Sheppard a gigantic favor...even if it got the stupid bastard killed.

But mostly it was about survival—Arthur Brock's—and what could happen to him if he let Ma down, did nothing, let it slide. Somehow, some way, the error of omission would come back to haunt him. At the very least, his flow of untaxed money from the 14K would be cut off, cold turkey, but he couldn't trust Ma to let it go at that. More likely, Ma would feel the need to make a fresh example of the cop who failed him, and that was the kind of lesson you didn't survive.

At first Brock figured—even hoped—that he was on a wild-goose chase, but damned if Mr. X hadn't gone back to Chinatown, just like a homing pigeon. Brock had paid off the taxi, walked back to the apartment building where Ma made his dirty movies and saw the stranger duck in from the street and disappear.

Brock didn't follow him inside, afraid of what was coming. He'd have no way to explain his presence at the scene if he was right. The lieutenant didn't hear the shooting, but he knew the guy was carrying because of a glimpse of hardware he'd gotten as the stranger had entered the apartment building from the street. Six minutes later, when he came downstairs and drove away, Brock waited, saw the dazed survivors straggling out and making tracks like they had caught a glimpse of Judgment Day and didn't plan on sitting through the main event.

Upstairs, he'd found a dead Chinese, bleeding from a scalp wound. Brock left the call to someone else and got out of there.

He walked four blocks and flagged another taxi, rode back to the Empire State Building and picked up his unmarked sedan. The drive back to his office gave him time to think about what he had seen, and what it meant to Terry Sheppard.

Somehow, Shep was working with the triggerman who had been giving Ma the fits all day. It was impossible to guess how they first met, what made the sergeant throw in with a screwball vigilante warrior, whether there were more than just the two of them involved. Brock's duty ended with a call to William Ma, and he would let the red pole handle it from there.

The mobile telephone in Brock's car was a little something special, purchased through a catalog for $19.95 plus tax. Aside from all the normal buttons, it had switches that employed computer wizardry to change a caller's voice. With the device in hand, a man could come off sounding like a woman or vice versa, six variations in all. Brock knew Ma's lines were tapped—hell, he was tapping them himself—but they wouldn't be using names, and with his special telephone, Intelligence, Narcotics, Vice—whoever—wouldn't have a prayer of matching voiceprints.

Ma knew all about the special telephone, of course. When he responded on the second ring, a sexy woman's voice advised the red pole that he had a message coming "from downtown." Another touch, and the lieutenant's baritone became a mellow tenor.

"This is me," he said. "I've got what you've been looking for. We need a face-to-face."

HAHN BROTHERS RANKED among the top investment firms in Chinatown, which was to say that it was one of two or three small companies that struggled in the shadow of Manhattan's main financial district, trading stocks and bonds, acquiring real estate for its discriminating clients. The books were tidy, scrupulously clean, and showed a modest profit every year, on which Hahn Brothers paid their taxes without pulling any fast ones on the IRS.

Or so it seemed.

There was another set of books for William Ma's investments through the firm, a flow of cash that made up forty-five percent of all the income brothers Mark and Michael Hahn secured within a given year. That was the forty-five percent that never showed up on their state and federal tax reports, and corresponded perfectly to the percentage of their company owned outright, through selected front men, by Ma.

Hahn Brothers was responsible for making Ma a closet millionaire with interests as diverse as Carolina textiles and tobacco, condominiums in Philadelphia, a chain of theaters in Illinois and several auto dealerships along the Eastern Seaboard. As for stocks and bonds, they put him in tax-free municipals and helped him buy a small but thriving segment of the information superhighway, staking out a corner of the software market with an emphasis on interactive CD-ROMs that ranged from children's fairy tales to hard-core porn for dear old Dad.

Hahn Brothers did most of its business on the telephone, deploring walk-ins at the third-floor office on Canal Street. Still, it happened now and then, as with the round-eye who arrived ten minutes short of closing time that afternoon and asked to speak with someone in authority.

Mark Hahn came out to see the stranger, covering reluctance with a practiced smile that only lost its shine when he beheld the Uzi submachine gun pointed at his face. With his receptionist, two brokers and the cleaning lady who had come in early to begin her work, Hahn walked back to the office where he kept the petty cash—three-quarters of a million dollars, give or take—locked up securely in a floor safe set beneath his antique hardwood desk.

"There must be some mistake," Hahn told the solemn gunner, trying to maintain his dignity despite the fact that he was kneeling on the carpet like a peon, stuffing bundled currency into a plastic garbage bag.

"I wouldn't be surprised," the white man told him. "You can talk it over with the IRS on Monday morning, if you're still in town. They got computer printouts on a few of your transactions with the 14K this afternoon, by special courier."

Hahn felt the building tilt, but knew that was crazy. He was simply taken by surprise that anyone outside of Chinatown—much less a white man—should know anything about his deal with William Ma. It was a toss-up, whether Hahn was more afraid of being shot or audited. He might survive a bullet wound; if not, at least his worldly troubles would be over when he died. The IRS was something else, though: an eternal plague, like AIDS or cancer, that would never let you go.

"That's everything," he said.

"Okay. You've got a weekend coming up. I wouldn't be surprised if you could make it down to Nassau, grab that money you've got stashed and get yourself some breathing room before the Feds show up."

A ray of hope... but was it real, or an illusion? Hahn suspected being spared from death wasn't the blessing it appeared to be. Someone would have to tell Ma about the robbery, at least, and give him a description of the thief. That was easy, in itself, unless Ma started asking questions, getting paranoid, suspecting Hahn and company of some collusion in the plot.

Hahn knew that he should call his brother first, put things in motion for their getaway, before he made the other call. In fact, he just might stall a bit, call Ma from someplace safer. Like the airport, just before his flight to the Bahamas finished boarding.

Yes.

He could already feel the tropic sunshine on his face. With any luck at all, it just might keep the hungry shadows out of range.

THE PORNO HIT on Pell was no big deal, considering what else had gone down that afternoon—one dead, a hard-core chicken hawk named Yehkun Chong, six years in the United States without a call to Immigration.

It was small potatoes on the surface, Terry Sheppard thought, but it showed Mike Blanski's grim determination to leave no potential nest of maggots hidden from the cleansing light of day in Chinatown. White Powder Ma would lose a few grand on the pad, equipment, personnel and shooting schedule—possibly a great deal more than that, if Vice was able to connect him with the studio directly.

Not much chance of that, Sheppard thought, as he put the seedy place behind him and walked back to the unmarked cruiser he had double-parked outside. He would have blown the call off in a second, but he wanted to see more of Blanski's work, try for an understanding of the big man's thinking, see what made him tick.

He had a hard-on for the 14K and Luk Pang, that much was obvious. But was it personal, or was he really working for some shadow agency behind the scenes, the holder of some off-the-record federal hunting license?

Did it matter?

Sheppard was surprised to answer that one in the negative. Against all odds, he found he didn't give a damn who Blanski's backers were, as long as it wasn't some other syndicate invading Ma's preserve to clinch a variation on the old-line status quo. His years in Chinatown had turned him as cynical as hell, and it was a relief to see a new broom sweeping out the trash, by any means available.

Sheppard felt the office calling him, a need to be close to the telephone when Blanski called him back. He had a lead on Luk Pang—still not an address, but a source that might, just might, reveal the information Blanski needed to complete his sweep.

He made a flagrantly illegal U-turn in the midst of traffic, switching on his flashing lights just long enough to pull it off, before he started south on Bowery, away from Chinatown. He missed the car that fell in close behind him as he left the scene, wrapped up in private thoughts, not concentrating on the rearview mirror. By the time they started shooting at him, he was half a mile from Pell Street, already imagining what he would say to Blanski when he got the call.

The first round was a hasty shot that drilled the left-rear fender of his drab four-door sedan. Somebody would catch hell for that one, later, but he didn't stop to think about it as he caught a flash of hardware in his mirror, ducking just in time to save himself from half a dozen well-placed rounds of automatic fire. His window shattered, raining glass down Sheppard's collar, then the bullets took out his windshield, sheared off the rearview and took a bite out of his steering wheel.

He stood on the accelerator, driving blind and waiting for the impact of a crash that would mean he was finished, trapped, pinned down. A sitting duck. The gunners kept pace with him, spraying bullets at the car, but they were mostly using hollowpoints, which failed to penetrate the Chrysler's bodywork. For something like a quarter of a second, he considered firing back, but knew he couldn't hit the broad side of the World Trade Center in the circumstances, picturing the flak he would face if he capped a civilian in broad daylight, racing down the street and pumping wild rounds out his window.

Screw it.

Sheppard concentrated on his driving, made it south as far as East Broadway, with Bowery turning into St. James Place, before he lost it. Crossing on the red, hunched down below the dash, he caught a city bus broadside and heard the Chrysler's engine go. It was a miracle he didn't wind up with the damned thing in his lap, another reason to be thankful the department bought American.

But he was stranded now. The gunners would be coming for him. Sheppard drew his service automatic, thumbed the hammer back, then released the safety harness that had saved him from a head butt with the dashboard. Groping for the handle of the passenger's door, he bailed out on that side, dropping to a crouch behind the ruined Chrysler. There was no more shooting, but he couldn't count his chickens. The eggs weren't even cool yet, much less hatching.

Sheppard risked a glance above the right-rear fender, peering out across the trunk, and found himself the center of a cursing, honking traffic jam. The shooters—had they been Chinese?—were gone, nothing besides the bullet holes in Sheppard's ride to prove that they had ever passed that way.

He rose, felt giddy with relief as he reached back inside the car to snare the two-way radio and call for help.

THE LOAN OFFICE on Mott Street didn't advertise in the business section of the Manhattan telephone directory. It didn't advertise at all, in fact, but rather got referrals from the street by word of mouth. It wasn't licensed with the state or city of New York, endured no audits or inspections by officialdom in any form. The loans weren't recorded with a recognized financial institution, nor were terms and interest rates controlled by any state or federal legislation, as was usual in such matters.

Bolan dawdled past the loan office, on the far side of the street, and watched as a gray-haired man dressed for the 1950s emerged from the entrance: gray suit, matching tie, fedora planted squarely on his head, like something from an early G-man film. Except that this man was Chinese, and Hoover's FBI had never welcomed Asians to the ranks with open arms.

This walking piece of history would be a local merchant, either taking out a loan or dropping off his latest payment to the shark. If it ran true to form, the short-term loans involved an interest rate of twenty-five to forty-five percent, compounded weekly, and the penalty for tardy payments ran toward gouged eyes, broken bones and catastrophic vandalism.

It was much the same in immigrant communities throughout the country and around the world. Each race or nationality included certain predators who victimized their own, cashed in on hardship and discrimination faced by their people in a foreign land. If native banks refused to authorize a loan for the expansion of small business, or to pay the passage of a loved one dearly missed, the desperate supplicant could always find someone with extra cash on hand, delighted to be helpful . . . for a price. Some failed to understand the terms when they received the money; others were so confident of this or that new enterprise that they could live with *any* rate of interest for a while; some others were so desperate for cash they would have promised anything on earth to break the sorry stalemate of their lives.

It all came out the same, when the collectors were dispatched to bring back money or a pound of flesh. In Little Italy, the loan-shark business was controlled by mafiosi, while the blacks and Puerto Ricans in their ghettos paid the tab to neighborhood enforcers linked to any one of a half-dozen well-armed gangs. In Little Tokyo, a kind of homegrown Yakuza had put down roots. In fact, no ethnic area or poor white neighborhood was free of parasites in human form, who victimized the needy and the greedy, seven days a week, year-round.

He had no way of judging who was in the office, customers and such, but Bolan didn't have the time to spare for loitering on Mott Street, when White Powder Ma had soldiers sweeping Chinatown in search of a suspicious-looking round-eye. Waiting for a gap in traffic, the Executioner crossed in the middle of the block and reached the curb two doors south of his target. Pushing through the door, he had the Uzi out and tracking, several Chinese gaping at him, startled at the presence of a seeming madman in their midst.

He counted five, three of them women. One man was a forty-something mobster type with manicured nails and frosty eyes behind a pair of gold-rimmed spectacles. His sidekick was a slugger in his early twenties, lean and mean, with slicked-back hair and a shiny suit—in short, the central casting version of a punk with "class." They glared at Bolan, while the women flanking them seemed undecided as to whether they should scream or simply cringe in silence from the man and weapon.

It might have been the women, or the presence of his boss, but something urged the punk to prove himself. He wasn't all that fast, but there was lethal hardware underneath his shiny jacket, and it would have been a grave mistake to let him draw. The Uzi whispered, three rounds punching through the gunner's chest, and he went down without a whimper, stretched out on the vinyl floor while crimson pooled beneath him, spreading rapidly.

One of the women did scream then, but her companions silenced her before she had a chance to make the stranger nervous. Meanwhile, the apparent man in charge was scrutinizing Bolan, working up the nerve to speak.

"Is this a robbery?" he asked. The frown he wore told Bolan that he knew what had been happening in Chinatown that afternoon.

"Not quite," the Executioner replied. "It's personal, between myself and William Ma. You're going out of business. What I need, right now, is someone who can show me where the records are."

"The records?"

"Of your loans," Bolan said. "Don't play dumb. It doesn't suit you."

"May the women leave?"

"By all means. They'd be wise to go straight home, not stop along the way for any phone calls, if you get my drift."

The man spoke briefly to his three female employees in Cantonese, and while he could have told them anything, it made no difference to Bolan. They could summon reinforcements if they liked. With any luck, he would be gone before a hit team could arrive. If not, he was prepared to deal with any opposition as it came.

The women left, avoiding Bolan's gaze with downcast eyes. His hostage waited until the door had closed behind them, then he turned and led the way into a private office at the back. Three filing cabinets stood against one wall, directly opposite a cluttered desk.

"The files," he said.

"That's everything? Outstanding debts and payment schedules? Nothing tucked away somewhere that I ought to know about?"

"That's all."

It hardly mattered, since the thermite would get everything, regardless. All the same, he took the extra time to open drawers in all three cabinets, placed one grenade on top of them and rolled another underneath the desk.

"We'd better split, unless you feel like going up in smoke."

Outside, the Uzi hidden underneath his coat, he spent another moment with the aging shark. "When you talk to Ma," Bolan said, "tell him I can keep this up all week, if necessary. What I want is Luk Pang, a termination of his dealings with the 14K. Can you remember that?"

"I can."

"Okay, so take a hike and make the call. Your boss is running out of time."

The loan shark had a certain phony dignity about him as he turned away and started walking north on Mott Street. Bolan headed in the opposite direction, toward his car, and he was rolling by the time smoke started belching from the late loan office.

Cleansing fire.

He wasn't finished yet, but he was getting warm.

THE C-4 PLASTIC CHARGE went off like distant thunder, muffled slightly by the intervening brick-and-concrete walls. A block south of the blast site, Bolan dropped the compact radio remote into his pocket, watching smoke begin to billow from the underground garage that served Ma's soldiers as a Triad motor pool. A couple of survivors staggered into daylight, gagging on the smoke and fumes of burning gasoline, one of them running for the nearest fire alarm to ring it in.

He walked back to the Mazda, motored northwest on Canal until he cleared the edge of Chinatown and started looking for a public telephone. A service station on his left met Bolan's needs, the phone booth tucked around in back, adjacent to the rest rooms. Bolan dropped a coin and tapped out Terry Sheppard's office number, waiting through four rings for a familiar voice.

"Sheppard."

"Can you talk?"

"Just barely," the detective told him, lowering his voice. "Some of your playmates nearly took me out on Bowery, about an hour ago. I have another conversation with the shooting team, here, any minute."

"You're all right?"

"So far. I can't imagine what they had in mind, unless . . ."

He left it hanging, but the gist of his concern was obvious. The only reason for Ma to waste a cop would be if he believed the target had betrayed him somehow. And since Sheppard wasn't on the Triad's payroll, that could only mean he was suspected of cooperating with Ma's enemies.

"You'll need to watch yourself," Bolan said, laying out the obvious.

"I got that message, thanks. You clear?"

"So far. I guess you haven't had a chance to check that other information."

"Au contraire, amigo," Sheppard answered, mixing up his languages deliberately. "I don't have any whereabouts on Pang himself, but I've got someone you could talk to, if you find him."

"Go ahead."

"Name's Philip Soo. He drives for Pang, and maybe does some other odd jobs. I wouldn't be surprised. He's got a place at Pell and Doyers, fifth floor, corner flat."

He memorized the address Sheppard gave him and repeated it for confirmation. There was little more to say. Repeated warnings would have been an insult to the cop's intelligence and a colossal waste of time.

"I'll be in touch," Bolan said.

"Better not. If I'm being shadowed here, you'll blow your act."

And that was true. The best thing he could do, for Sheppard and himself, was break it off.

"You're right," he agreed, and cradled the receiver softly.

13

Dusk had turned to full-fledged night in Chinatown, as Bolan started hiking west on Pell from Bowery, toward the Doyers intersection. He knew all about the history of Bloody Corner, and hoped it wouldn't have to live up to that rep this night, but he was ready to proceed with any means required to find Luk Pang and bring his house down.

Any means at all.

He had a physical description of his target, the address and Sheppard's warning that the man he sought was seldom—some said never—found to be unarmed. That posed no special problem, in itself, unless he had an army with him, and the odds of that were small indeed. The greater risk, as Bolan realized, was that Soo would already have split, to hide with Luk Pang, and thus deprive him of the opportunity for some constructive interrogation.

Still, he could only work with what he had, and if he failed, it wouldn't be from lack of trying. Bolan reached the intersection, found the address he was looking for and went in through the front as if he owned the place.

The lobby was a dingy, dwarfish space, no larger than the men's room at a cut-rate filling station. Banks of mailboxes stood on Bolan's left as he went in, a vase of dusty plastic flowers on his right. He spurned the antique elevator and took the chance of meeting someone on the stairs as he began his swift ascent.

The whole place smelled like food, with cabbage out in front, but it didn't whet Bolan's appetite. A very different hunger drove him up the stairs, ten flights with threadbare carpet underfoot and dim bulbs on the landings for his only light. Approaching four, he brought the Uzi out of hiding, just in case.

On five, he half expected soldiers, but the corridor was empty. Bolan started at the far end from his destination, moving cautiously as he approached the corner flat that would, he guessed, provide the best view in the house of Bloody Corner down below.

He paused and listened briefly at the door. Faint sounds of laughter came from within, sounding more like television than real life. That meant there was somebody home, but he couldn't begin to guess how many, who they were or how they might be armed. For that, he had to get inside and have a look around.

There was a point where caution changed to procrastination—doubt and fear creeping in to stay a warrior's hand, and sometimes cost his life, if he delayed too long. Instead of waiting any longer, for the sound of living voices and a chance to gauge the hostile force he would be facing, Bolan took his chances, kicked the door in and followed in a rush.

A solitary man stood gaping at him, with a bowl of popcorn in one hand, a beer can in the other. His appearance matched the physical description Bolan had received of Philip Soo. The automatic pistol tucked inside his waistband banished any latent doubts.

Soo had his hands full, but he tried to play it cool as Bolan heeled the front door shut behind him. Holding out the plastic bowl of popcorn toward his uninvited guest, he said, "You want some?"

Bolan was about to answer, when the beer can hurtled toward his face. He ducked the foaming missile, saw his adversary drop the bowl of popcorn as he started reaching for the autoloader at his waste. It was a tricky kind of shot to make, when you were in a hurry, but he stroked the Uzi's trigger lightly, aiming low, and cut Soo's legs from under him with half a dozen parabellum rounds.

The Chinese gunner landed on his back, teeth clenched around the cud of pain, still trying for the handgun. Bolan's second burst opened up Soo's shoulder like an ax blade slicing seasoned wood. Soo shuddered with the impact and the pain, but didn't scream. Instead, it looked like he was lapsing into shock.

That wouldn't do for Bolan's purposes. He didn't care if Philip Soo survived or not, but he had to find out what the gunman knew of Luk Pang's whereabouts. He moved in closer, tossed the pistol out of reach and dragged his wounded adversary toward the couch. Instead of lifting Soo onto the cushions, Bolan hauled him upright, none too gently, so he sat with shoulders braced against the sofa, with his backside on the floor.

"You're hurt," he told the man, "but nothing they can't fix. You want to live, I have one question for you. Simple. Do we understand each other?"

"Fuck yourself, white man." Despite the pain and shock, Soo's voice was strong and steady.

Bolan did the only thing he could, under the circumstances. He delivered a hammer blow to the man's wounded shoulder. Before Soo had a chance to scream, the Executioner clasped one hand tight across his adversary's mouth, the other probing with the Uzi's muzzle, at his groin.

"You're getting whittled down," Bolan said. "How much is it worth to you, for Pang to skate while you take all the lumps?"

He drew his hand away to let Soo answer, braced for anything from screams to snapping teeth, but what he got was answers, in a different tone.

"He went to Staten Island, New Dorp, with Ma. The red pole has a house on Hylan Boulevard, by Great Kills Park. Don't know the number."

That would be the least of Bolan's problems, he decided, as he backed off and rose from his crouch as he prepared to leave. Soo might be lying to him, but he didn't think so. There was anger in his eyes—and something else.

"One thing, before you go," the gunner said.

"What's that?" Bolan asked.

"Finish it. My betrayal will get me killed, anyway."

It was the least that he could do. Another burst, from fifteen feet, and he was out of there, jogging back to his car, before the long drive out to Staten Island.

Great Kills Park.

He only hoped the place would live up to its name.

"It's NOT MY FAULT, goddamn it!"

Arthur Brock was losing patience with the whole damned thing, and getting more than slightly nervous, if the truth was known. He had agreed to visit William Ma at the red pole's estate on Staten Island, where the man had gone to ground, but that had been a courtesy. No way had Brock intended for the meeting to become some kind of frigging inquisition, with himself as the accused. It wasn't *his* men who had blown the hit on Terry Sheppard. *He* wasn't the one responsible for putting Ma's ass in the ringer, squeezing him until he bleated like a frigging billy goat.

"You were supposed to help us," Ma reminded him, a sharp edge in his voice.

"I did, for God's sake. It was me who told you Sheppard's name and where to find him for the hit, remember? I connected him with this guy who's been ragging you all over town. It's not my fault your men can't nail him down, when they've got odds of four or five to one in broad daylight."

"My soldiers have been disciplined," Ma said. "It doesn't solve the problem we all face."

"Who's 'we'?" Brock asked him. "No one's after me."

"They will be, if my problems aren't resolved," Ma told him. "I detest incompetence, Lieutenant, and I will not stand for insubordination. You are paid—and very handsomely, at that—to help with problems of this nature. So far, you've been less than helpful, yes?"

"I told you—"

"It is not enough," Ma interrupted him. "The actions of our enemy in Chinatown are both embarrassing and costly. In the present circumstances, I cannot afford to pay employees who do not perform. You understand?"

"I hear you."

"It is cheaper and more satisfying to—how do you say it—cut my losses?"

"Wait a second now..."

"There's no time left," Ma told him. "If you cannot help me, you are useless. I do not keep useless things."

Brock glanced from Ma to Luk Pang and back again. The two of them were staring at him like he was some kind of sideshow freak or something, neither of them looking worried, as they should have been, when they were threatening a veteran NYPD officer with death.

The lieutenant understood that they could kill him where he sat, and nobody would know the difference. His wife thought he was working on some kind of stakeout, and the brass downtown would figure he was at home, if they gave any thought to him at all. The only people in the world that knew his present whereabouts were Chinese gangsters who would rather cut their own tongues out than squeal on William Ma.

"What is it that you want from me?" he asked, his tone more reasonable now, less strained.

"Results," Pang said, the first time he had spoken since they took their seats around the low-slung coffee table in Ma's den.

"I'm doing what I can," Brock replied, "but I can try and turn up the heat under Sheppard, get him cooking on this thing. That way, he'll be exposed, you know? Your guys can pick him off, unless they fuck it up again.''

''There will be no more careless errors,'' Ma replied, ''unless you make them.''

''Well, in that case—''

Brock was rising from his chair, more than a little anxious to be on his way, when a staccato burst of gunfire echoed from the grounds. He felt the blood drain from his face, already riffling through his mental file of logical excuses for an answer that would satisfy when IA asked him what in holy hell he had been doing at the home of a suspected narco dealer when the shit went down.

Of course, if he could get away before the uniforms arrived, then it would all be cool.

''I'll check that out,'' he volunteered, a beat too quickly.

''No!'' Ma bolted to his feet and aimed a bony index finger at Brock's chest, as if it were a weapon. ''You stay here. We may have need of a policeman tonight.''

In his mind, Brock heard a flushing sound and saw his pension going down the crapper, just like that. He had to get the hell away from Ma and company, if he was going to survive this and there was no time to finesse the move.

With grim determination, Brock reached for the .38 Chief's Special on his hip.

THERE WAS an outside chance the sentry could have lived to see the sun rise, but a deviation from his beat brought him directly into Bolan's path and sealed his fate. The silenced Uzi made no sound to speak of, opening the gunner's chest, but even with an instant kill there was a risk of some reflexive action on the target's part. In this case, with the sentry carrying an MP-5 K submachine gun, that meant one long burst of aimless automatic fire before he hit the deck and lost his weapon.

And the one burst was enough.

It had been relatively easy, slipping into William Ma's estate on Staten Island. The original construction had been done with fashion rather than security in mind, a compromise that made the stone wall scalable without a need for specialized equipment. There were no surveillance cameras on the wall or in the trees beyond, no motion sensors on the grounds to pick up footsteps. Ma put his faith in men with guns and scattered them around the property on foot patrol. Their walkie-talkies whispered in the darkness, sometimes hissing static, helping Bolan find them—or avoid them—when they should have concentrated more on ways to make things difficult for a potential enemy.

He was avoiding them by choice and moving closer to the house, more interested in finding Ma and Pang than in a skirmish with the troops, when one of Ma's young soldiers blundered off the beaten track and it began to fall apart. Within a moment of the wild airburst, he heard a dozen gunners closing on him, shouting back and forth or speaking into their radios as they advanced. No firing yet, but it wouldn't take long once they began to look for targets in the shadows.

Time to move, and he couldn't afford to let them pin him down. Retreat across the wall would blow his last, best chance of nailing Pang before the ChiCom activist could flee New York for parts unknown, and Bolan didn't mean to let him slip away again.

They had been playing tag across the continent for three days now, and it was time to bring down the curtain, move on into the next phase of the killing game.

He palmed a frag grenade and armed it, held the lethal egg in his right hand as he took off in the direction of the house. He ran a zigzag course, avoiding several of the gunners even as they passed him in the darkness, running headlong toward the source of recent gunfire.

Easy.

But he couldn't dodge them all. The Executioner wasn't invisible, nor could he cast a magic spell on his opponents. Coming up in front of him, a group of three were running on a hard collision course, and dodging them would only throw him back into the middle of the pack.

So be it.

Bolan lobbed the grenade and stepped into the shelter of an oak tree large enough to soak up any shrapnel from the blast. It wasn't perfect cover, but it was the best available, and he would make the most of what he had.

They never saw it coming, ran into the rending, tearing flash like stuntmen in a movie, shattered bodies vaulting through the air and crashing down in broken heaps of flesh and bone. The blast eliminated any final hope of slipping past the palace guard, but it confused them for a moment, smoke and echoes, cries of pain and startled curses throwing his pursuers briefly off the track.

He took advantage of the moment, charging toward the house, his submachine gun ready for the soldiers who would certainly be waiting there to head him off.

If they were green enough to let him take them by surprise, or scared enough to flinch before they started pulling triggers, Bolan still might have a chance. In any case, he had to try his best, keep going toward the goal line, recognizing that he was beyond the point of no return.

It was a case of do or die, and Bolan knew that it could still go either way.

WILLIAM MA couldn't believe the stupid cop was actually reaching for his gun, but there it was, the stubby .38 revolver waving back and forth between himself and Pang.

"I'm walking out of here," Brock said. "It wouldn't be the best idea you ever had to try and stop me."

"This is a mistake," Ma told him, edging back in the direction of his desk. "We are your friends."

"Yeah, right." Brock's voice was scornful.

"I've paid you well for services received," Ma said, as he sat behind the desk. "The choice was always yours."

"Damn right it was," Brock said, "and now I'm choosing not to play, all right? Nobody *owns* me, get it? You can shove that red pole garbage up your ass, for all I care. I'm history."

"Indeed."

Ma's fingers closed around the pistol hidden underneath his desk, a .45-caliber Glock 21. The gun was cocked and locked, his finger on the trigger all that was required to switch off the special safety and pump three rounds at Brock, directly through the forward panel of Ma's desk.

At least one bullet found its mark. The man staggered, squeezing off a wild shot from his .38 that struck the wall above Ma's head. Ma had the automatic braced in both hands now, sighting across the desktop, and he pumped two bullets into the lieutenant's chest. Brock lost his weapon, clutching at the crimson pattern soaking through his shirt, and tumbled backward to the floor.

"He must have been insane to threaten me in my own home," Ma said. Pang stared at him, impassive, as the dead man's blood began to soak the carpet.

"That will have to be replaced," Ma said, already moving toward the exit from his den. A soldier poked his head in, brandishing a weapon, visibly relaxing when he saw the round-eye dead, his master standing tall above the corpse.

"What's happening outside?" Ma asked.

"I don't know," the guard replied. "Somebody started shooting."

"Obviously. Go and see what—"

The explosion silenced Ma. He glanced at Pang, saw fear on his companion's face and drew strange comfort from the sight. Communists were long on theory, after all, but they weren't real fighting men. When it came down to killing, they still needed help from the professionals.

"I want the car at once," Ma told his gunner. "Have it brought around back. We won't be long."

"Yes, sir."

The soldier disappeared to carry out his orders. It would take some time, of course, to get the driver moving, fetch the Lincoln Town Car out of the garage and get it in position. Time enough for Ma to fill his briefcase with the money, passport and assorted other items he kept ready in his wall safe for emergencies. The Lincoln had a mobile telephone; they could arrange for airline tickets once they cleared the battle zone and started driving north, in the direction of the Verrazano Narrows Bridge. From there, it was a smooth run through the heart of Brooklyn, into Queens, where they would have their choice of airports.

Simple.

But they had to reach the car first. That, Ma realized, would be the tricky part, with hostile gunmen on the grounds. If necessary, he would sacrifice Pang to save himself, but there was still a chance it wouldn't come to that. If they were swift enough. If all went well.

Ma finished cleaning out his safe and snapped the briefcase shut. Pang watched him with wary eyes, hands clasped behind his back. The man wasn't armed—he had been frisked upon arrival, by Ma's soldiers—but he still had a suspicious look about him.

Ma choked down the feeling of uneasiness and forced a smile.

"I'm going now," he told Pang, moving toward the door. "Would you prefer to wait and greet our guests, or will you join me in the car?"

CALL IT WHIM OR INSTINCT, expectation or experience. Before he reached the house and came in range of gunners waiting there, behind the floodlights, Bolan knew that he would be outnumbered if he rushed the door directly. That wasn't enough to stop him, but neither was the soldier's style to throw his life away on empty gestures that gained nothing for his cause. If he could leave them waiting for him there, and come in from the back instead, he still might have a fighting chance.

It meant a deviation in his course, a longer run, but that was nothing to complain about. Behind him, in the trees, Ma's guards had started shooting one another, flashlight beams and muzzle-flashes stabbing through the darkness, tracking man-size shadows on the killing ground.

He ran, letting the darkness cover him as long as it was able, looping wide around the house to come in from the back. It was illogical to think that there would be no sentries in the rear, but with the action going on out front, he stood a decent chance of seeing any major opposition drawn away to join the fight. If they weren't commanded to pitch in, he knew from private battlefield experience, a fair percentage would slip off to join the action on their own, afraid of missing out or being labeled cowards if they weren't involved in spilling blood.

Bolan reached his jumping-off point, lingered in the shadows of the tree line for a moment, checking out his target. He saw a Lincoln Town Car pulling out of the garage and rolling slowly toward the back door of the house, where two young soldiers waited for it like valets with automatic weapons. Bolan didn't have to guess which member of the household had authority to order up a car while soldiers were dying on the grounds outside.

William Ma was bailing out.

It stood to reason Luk Pang would join him, if the ChiCom operative was even there. So far, he had only the word of Philip Soo to guide him, and there was a chance—however slim—that he had been deceived. In that case, he would have to settle for the red pole's head and start from scratch in seeking Pang, once he escaped from Ma's estate.

He stayed in place another moment and saw more men emerging from the house. Another soldier led the way, with

Ma immediately on his heels. Behind Ma, looking tired and harried, Luk Pang glanced left and right, as if expecting to be ambushed where he stood.

And he was right.

They didn't see him coming, the soldiers concentrating on the sounds of combat emanating from the far side of the house, as Bolan charged them from the tree line, sprinting toward the car. The nearest guard still had his back to Bolan when a burst of parabellum manglers clipped his spine below the shoulder blades and pitched him forward, sprawling facedown on the pavement.

That was all it took to ruin the surprise, but he was closing on them now, and there was little they could do about it. Two armed sentries and the driver gaped at him, the soldiers bringing up their weapons while the driver yelped and threw himself behind the Lincoln's steering wheel. Pang and Ma looked dazed, uncomprehending.

Bolan took the next shooter with a quick burst to the face and watched his head explode on impact. Blood and chunks of brain were spattered on his comrade's face, half blinding him, and there was no time for a wipe-down in the circumstances. Firing aimlessly, the final gunner tried to hide behind the car, but he was just a beat too slow. Nine millimeter bullets punched him over backward. Dying as he fell, his finger clenched around the trigger of his submachine gun, he wasted half a magazine on stars and sky.

That still left three, and Bolan knew all of them were dangerous. He took the driver first, before the guy could put his ride in gear and peel out with a screech of rubber. Firing through the tinted right-hand window, Bolan nailed his target with a 4-round burst and left him slumped across the wheel.

Ma and Pang were in the back seat of the car, prepared to flee, when Bolan killed their driver. Ma bailed out immediately, brandishing a semiauto pistol, squeezing off two shots at the Executioner in a rush that made them both go high and wide. He answered with a burst from the Uzi that tattooed holes across the red pole's chest and dropped him like a boneless scarecrow on the pavement.

Luk Pang saw how the tide had shifted, felt it sucking at his feet, but he wasn't the kind of man who passively surrendered to defeat. Unarmed, he threw himself against the door away from Bolan's side, spilled out on hands and knees, but swiftly scrambled to his feet and started to run, following the driveway as it looped around the house and out of sight.

Too late.

The Uzi sputtered, and a burst of parabellum shockers lifted Pang completely off his feet, a hurdle jumper flailing with his arms and legs before the pull of gravity returned and brought him crashing down. His body twitched and quivered for a moment, seemed about to rise again, but then the life ran out of him and he was still.

Which left the Executioner to face a small but angry private army on his own, with no one in authority to call them off.

He slammed the rear doors of the Lincoln Town Car, dragged out the lifeless driver, and took his place. The seat was slick with blood beneath him, soaking through his blacksuit, but discomfort was the least of Bolan's problems at the moment. Rolling out of there, he had to gamble that the troops would hesitate before they fired upon their leader's vehicle. The night, confusion and tinted windows all combined to hide his round-eyed face from those who would have killed him instantly if they had seen a white man in the driver's seat.

The tall front gates were open, waiting for him when he got there, one guard bending down and blinking at him through the shattered window on his right.

Tough luck.

He would have ditched the Lincoln and retrieved his own car by the time they organized a viable pursuit. His business in New York was finished, but the war wasn't.

The Executioner was moving on.

14

London, England

The transatlantic flight from JFK to Gatwick, outside London, ate up seven hours once the giant 747 finally got airborne. It was a commercial flight, as no military lift was available, and Bolan had to travel light. There was no thought of concealing weapons in his luggage, even with the vaunted Northern Ireland cease-fire in effect. British authorities had learned about terrorism the hard way, since 1969, and they weren't about to let their guard down now because the IRA and rival Protestant guerrillas briefly laid their guns aside. Assuming it worked out—and Bolan wished them well in that regard—the Britons, especially in London, still had good and ample cause to fear a list of active terrorists that ranged from neo-Nazis on the right to crazy Maoists on the left, with everything from Scottish separatists to outlaw Palestinians caught in between.

He had a source for hardware waiting for him on the other side, and that would be the least of Bolan's problems when he hit the ground in London. Luk Pang was dead, and while he cherished no illusions that the 14K had been eradicated in the States or Canada by his campaign, the scene was changing on him now. Another, very different battleground was waiting, with the enemy entrenched and turning multimillion-dollar profits every day, year-round, on heroin, illegal aliens and black-market Chinese weapons.

From territorial disputes that led to public bloodshed in the latter 1970s, the list of Triad chiefs in London had been whittled down to one, a scar-faced "businessman" whose thousand-dollar suits and hundred-dollar haircuts hid a pirate's soul. Kam had battled to the top in London's Chinatown, and he had managed it without a single criminal conviction on his record—this despite the fact that he was linked, in confidential Scotland Yard reports, to more than thirty murders in the past five years. As London's red pole of the 14K, Wong Kam also controlled the bulk of China white that found its way to London and beyond, with customers in Birmingham and Leeds, Manchester, Cornwall, some as far away as Belfast.

It stood to reason that Kam would have a vested interest in his Triad's late cooperation with the Beijing government, especially where trade in Chinese immigrants and military hardware was concerned, but no one had identified his ChiCom counterpart in London, yet. That would be part of Bolan's task, and he would have a rather narrowly restricted hunting ground. In London, Chinatown was crammed into the southeast corner of Soho, around Gerrard Street, south of Shaftesbury Avenue, and while Chinese were free to live wherever they desired throughout the city, Bolan knew the Triad's operations would be concentrated there, as always, in the middle of the immigrant community.

It was a starting point, at least, and if he had to branch out later, seek his targets elsewhere, then he would follow where the blood spoor led him.

First, though, he would have to rent a car and touch base with the arms supplier recommended by his friends at Stony Man. A Sikh who ran a coin shop in the shadow of the King's Cross railway station, Bolan's contact had a stockpile of matériel on hand, and the soldier's shopping list was covered for the price of £7,000. Not bad, considering that it was Triad money, lifted from his adversaries in Vancouver and New York. He still had plenty in reserve, his second suitcase packed with cash, and Bolan wouldn't hesitate to spend it bringing down his enemies.

He wondered if Wong Kam and company were waiting for him, finally deciding there was no way they could guess where he would go—if anywhere—from New York City. Trouble in the States didn't translate to bloodshed in the streets of London, but he could expect the red pole to be on his guard, aware of what had happened in America, determined to protect himself and his domain at any cost.

In short, the usual.

Well armed and rested from his nap in flight, the Executioner went looking for his brand-new war.

"HE HASN'T ASKED for help yet," Hal Brognola said, "but you know Striker. He could be ass-deep in alligators, and he wouldn't say a word."

"He'd come out wearing alligator shoes," said Yakov Katzenelenbogen, facing the big Fed across the table in the War Room.

"Maybe so," Brognola answered, "but he's still no Superman."

"He doesn't know we're coming, right?" David McCarter's smile had more to do with irony and skepticism than amusement.

"Does it matter?" Brognola asked.

"Very possibly. I'd hate to drop in on him unannounced and get my arse shot off."

"You won't be joining him in London," he informed the men of Phoenix Force. "I want you waiting for him when he hits the continent, specifically in Amsterdam. The Triads have been having things their own way there for twenty years. It's time to bring them down a peg or two."

"Suppose he doesn't get to Amsterdam," McCarter asked, voicing the question each man present had already asked himself in private.

"Then you pick up where he dropped the ball and carry on alone. Is that a problem?"

"No," McCarter said.

"No problem," Katz chimed in, "but I would hate to see it go that way."

"We all would," Brognola said. "Anyway, let's focus on the positive. He's cleared three cities in as many days, and he eliminated the ChiCom connection in New York—which means the link for North America. They can't shrug that off in Beijing, and it's a safe bet that the 14K is hurting nationwide. I'd say we've made a decent start."

"I'm more concerned with how we finish," Katzenelenbogen said.

"The Triads make you nervous?" McCarter asked, grinning.

"No more than a hungry white shark in a swimming pool," the gruff Israeli answered. "I'd be happier if we had some idea of who was running this behind the scenes."

"No help on that, yet, I'm afraid," Brognola said. "The Britons were working on it, out of Hong Kong, but they lost their man in place. Before the guy got burned—I mean that literally, by the way—he told his handler he was checking into someone or something called the Red Dragon. Whether it's a code name for an individual, a group or some specific covert operation, well, your guess would be as good as mine."

"In other words," McCarter said, "we're working blind."

"Not quite. We know Beijing has cut a bargain with the 14K. The Triad's got carte blanche for weapons, drugs, illegal aliens—in short, whatever turns a profit for them in the West. The Reds don't cut a deal like that unless they're getting something in return."

"Specifics?" McCarter asked.

"We believe the 14K has been responsible for executing several Chinese dissidents abroad, including one in London last July. Chinese newspapers in the States and Western Europe have been catching hell the past twelve months or so for editorials on human rights at home. Bomb threats and vandalism, a grenade attack in Singapore, an editor beat up and slashed with razors in L.A. It's hard to prove conspiracy, of course, but I'm no great believer in coincidence with things like that."

"And spying?" Katzenelenbogen asked.

"Why not? Between illegal aliens and lawful immigrants who still have relatives in China, you've got thousands—millions—of potential eyes and ears collecting anything of interest to Beijing. A lot of people thought J. Edgar Hoover was a paranoid fanatic in the fifties when he lobbied for a cap on Chinese immigration to reduce the threat of spying, and I won't deny he was a senile bigot... but he may have had a point, regardless. Castro dumped a ton of problems on us with the boatlift back in 1980, but at least he did it in broad daylight. We could see the problem coming. With the traffic in illegals, well, you don't know what you're getting, since they're not on anybody's books."

"You think elimination of specific Triad leaders and their ChiCom contacts will reverse the trend?" Katz asked.

"I think we need to make a start," Brognola said. "I don't expect to solve the problem, granted, but we'll never see the end of it unless we draw the line somewhere. You know the attitude in Congress, since the USSR fell apart—'What Communists? What spies? What threat?' Those guys spent so much time and energy despising Russia for the better part of eighty years, it's slipped their mind that we've got other enemies alive and well out there."

"In Amsterdam," McCarter said, with no apparent irony.

"Consider it one cog in the machine," Brognola replied. "We've done some damage as it is—or, Striker has—but the machine's still functional. If we relax too soon, it stands to chew us up and spit us out."

Katz's voice was solemn as he asked, "When do we leave?"

Macau

THE DRAGON STOOD in darkness, staring at the distant lights of Hong Kong, with a wide expanse of pitch-black water in between. He pictured Edward Wong at home and hoped the leader of the 14K was also losing sleep over the recent troubles that had stricken them in North America.

Where would it end?

The Dragon had no answer to that vital question. Part of him wished he could take the field, as in the old days, and go looking for the enemy himself. It would be good to hunt again, instead of idling at the center of the hive and waiting for his drones to do the work, fetching back reports of their success or failure.

It was mostly failure, recently, at least in the United States and Canada. He hoped the virus wouldn't spread to other territories, but the Dragon's confidence had suffered in the past three days. So many soldiers dead, and while most of them had been Triads—mercenary bandits helping out the Dragon's cause for profit—he had also lost Luk Pang, together with a handful of loyal agents in the States.

It was a most unfortunate beginning to the next phase of their scheme. How could they ever hope to dominate the world, if they were massacred and driven out of scattered cities by an enemy who had no name, no face?

A lesser man would already have given up, but Cheung Kuo had never backed off from a battle once the fight was joined. He had been too much for the People's Army, as a young commander in the field—demanding too much of his troops, they said, as if a soldier of the revolution could be asked to give too much. Intelligence was more his field, the brass hats thought, where he could use his genius on a global scale, move spies and contract on the giant chessboard of the modern world.

And he had served his masters well...until this week. The failure wasn't his, of course, but Kuo accepted full responsibility for anything that happened under his command. A general who let his soldiers run amok or flee from danger like a pack of frightened children was a peril to his nation and the very troops who served him. When it came down to assessing blame, the Dragon would accept his share without complaint—no lame excuses to avoid the wrath of his superiors.

But he could mitigate their anger, try to save the situation even now, before it was too late. His agents were already working overtime to purge the paper trail of Luk Pang, eliminate the risk of Pang's name being traced back to Beijing. The dead man's Chinese origins couldn't be masked, of course, but there was no official link to any section of the mainland government, no cause for diplomatic protest from the States. One more illegal had come to grief, and who could say with any certainty what he was doing in America?

As for the 14K, he would leave Edward Wong to cope with any aftershocks from the chaotic violence of the past three days. The Dragon's own superiors believed that Pang and company had been caught up in some new gang war. It annoyed them, but the unadulterated truth—that nameless round-eyes were involved, perhaps with some official sanction from the U.S. government—would certainly have panicked them. Kuo was doing them a favor, he believed, by keeping that grim information to himself.

At least for now.

If he couldn't resolve the situation shortly, he would have to share the truth, and that would cast doubt on his credibility, no matter how he tried to make it sound like recent information. His masters weren't fools, by any means. They understood that field reports were sometimes cunning works of fiction, but it mattered little if the team was winning.

When they started losing, though, it was a very different game. In that case, explanations were demanded, and they had to fit the facts. Responsibility was weighed and measured, punishment decreed for those who failed to carry out appointed tasks in timely fashion.

There was no escape from judgment, if the game went wrong.

Which meant that Kuo would have to make it right, and soon, before the brass hats started asking those uncomfortable questions. He could use a rousing victory—or blessed peace and quiet, at the very least—to help erase the bloody memories of recent failure.

Even so, he reckoned it was lucky that the raids had taken place in North America, the wrong end of the pipeline, as it were. The States and Canada were one vast market, dumping ground, experimental station—take your pick—for schemes and products that originated in the East and flowed through Europe. It was fortunate for all concerned that their unknown, elusive enemies hadn't attacked in Amsterdam or London, for example, much less in the vital staging grounds of Bangkok and the Golden Triangle, Hong Kong, the Philippines.

In spite of everything, the Dragon thought they had been fortunate indeed.

Things could have been much worse.

London

THE TINY CHEMIST'S SHOP on Lisle Street, a block south of Gerrard, resembled any other Chinese drugstore, from Kowloon to the streets of San Francisco. Its proprietor didn't dispense prescriptions in the normal sense, wasn't a licensed pharmacist and probably had no more formal education than the average cabdriver passing on the street outside. The shop dealt mostly in what Westerners would call "home remedies," the herbs and potions drawn from nature that Chinese had used to treat their ills for several thousand years. Some of the items held in stock were perfectly mundane, such as ginseng, assorted berries, fungi, oils and lotions, while some others were "exotic" to the point of being banned by law: powdered rhinoceros horn and slices of dried tiger's penis, to help restore virility; various insects, serpents and mammalian embryos preserved in jars of alcohol; elixirs aimed at everything from infertility to cancer, epilepsy, AIDS and athlete's foot.

This particular shop offered something extra to its special customers, however, in the form of opium and heroin from Southeast Asia's Golden Triangle. The trade was brisk, in spite of British laws and policy that had largely decriminalized narcotics, since many addicts were unwilling to expose themselves by seeking treatment or transacting business at an outlet owned and operated by the government. Whether from ego or denial, fear of repercussions in the family or on the job, too many addicts still sought out illicit dealers, sometimes paying for their privacy with death or untold suffering.

Illegal heroin still earned a fortune for the Chinese Triads operating out of London, and that kind of money tempted rash competitors to horn in on the action. Albert Ming had owned the chemist's shop on Lisle Street for seven years, and he wouldn't unlock the door for business in the morning without armed guards on the premises to protect his inventory and himself. He had no special enemy in mind, but creeping paranoia was the price one paid for living on the wrong side of the law.

A fair percentage of Ming's customers were round-eyes, and he wasn't terribly surprised that morning when a white man walked into the shop, ignoring merchandise displayed on wooden shelves around him, and proceeded to the register where Ming was waiting.

"You're the pharmacist?" he asked.

"I am," Ming told him, putting on the smile he sometimes practiced in the mirror.

The pistol seemed to come from nowhere, fitted with the black tube of a silencer and aimed directly at the druggist's face. Ming felt his scrotum shrivel, short hairs bristling on his nape.

"You've got a button underneath the counter, I imagine," the white man said.

"Button?"

"For the soldiers. Go ahead and call them."

He was crazy, this one. Ming slid one hand underneath the counter, near the register, and did as he was told. There was no sound, but he could almost see the red light flashing in the back room, where his bodyguards sat smoking cigarettes and playing cards, surrounded by his stock of legal and illegal drugs.

Another moment, and he heard them coming in a rush, two men not even half his age. The young ones lusted after trouble, looking for an opportunity to prove their manhood in a way no female could accommodate. The stranger turned to face them, had them covered as the two of them came thrashing through the beaded curtain, guns in hand.

And it was over in a heartbeat, muffled coughing noises from the automatic in the white man's fist, Ming's two protectors going down together in a tangled sprawl of arms and legs. Their weapons clattered on the floor, one of them sliding into contact with Ming's foot. He thought of reaching for it, glanced back at the white man and saw death in those eyes.

"Your choice," the stranger said. "Just make it quick. I haven't got all day."

Ming raised his empty hands and stepped back from the weapon, fairly confident his next breath, or the next one after that, would be his last.

His captor nodded toward the beaded curtain at Ming's back and said, "You keep your stash in there?"

Ming nodded, waiting for the bullet that would drill a hole between his eyes. Instead of shooting him, however, the white man reached underneath his rain coat and took out a metal cylinder that Ming took several seconds to identify.

Some kind of hand grenade, but not the kind you saw in movies. He was staring as the stranger pulled the safety pin, then stepped closer to the door that served his storeroom.

"Do you want to live?" he asked.

Ming nodded, speechless with relief.

"Tell Scarface Kam that this is the beginning. I'm just getting started. He's got hell to pay, and I've been sent from the collection agency. You got that?"

"Yes."

"In that case, I suggest you hit the bricks, unless you're wearing flame-retardant underwear."

Ming fled the shop, not waiting for the muffled *whump* of the incendiary bomb that turned his shop into a blazing wreck, consuming heroin, home remedies, the two dead soldiers—everything. He didn't turn to watch the stranger go, but kept on running west on Lisle Street until he got to Wardour, the western edge of Chinatown.

He had to find a telephone and warn his master quickly, or he might be punished for his negligence. It hadn't been three minutes since the round-eyed gunman walked into his shop, yet everything had changed for Albert Ming. His life would never be the same.

He would transmit the warning, as demanded by his enemy, and Ming would wish his red pole well. But something told him it was already too late for Scarface Kam.

THE HARDWARE WASN'T Bolan's normal gear, but it would do. His new assault rifle was the 5.56 mm Individual Weapon issued as standard equipment to British ground troops, a bullpup design that measured thirty inches overall and offered a cyclic rate of fire in the neighborhood of 700 rounds per minute, with the 30-round detachable box magazine situated behind the pistol grip. The SUSAT optical sight was standard on British IWs, giving the weapon the look of a high-tech sniper rifle.

For greater concealment, he had also purchased a Heckler & Koch MP-5 K machine pistol, 12.8 inches overall, with a plastic foregrip underneath the stubby muzzle, boasting a full-auto cyclic rate of 800 rounds per minute in 9 mm parabellum. His side arm, with a threaded muzzle to accommodate a silencer, was the Browning BDA-9S manufactured by Fabrique Nationale. Spare ammo, magazines and various explosives rounded out the arsenal that Bolan carried with him in his rental car, as he proceeded toward the next address on his abbreviated hit list.

Driving north on Newport Place, he turned into an alleyway and found a place to park behind the Shi-liu Club, a Triad gambling house that would be opening for business in an hour or so. It was among the largest nondrug moneymakers Wong Kam had in Chinatown, ignored by Scotland Yard as long as no one beefed about the tables being rigged. If cash changed hands with the authorities, it was a simple cost of doing business in the modern world.

He went in through the back, the door unlocked as if he were expected. The custodian who met him was an older man, armed only with a push broom and a glare that might have worked on children. In the face of Bolan's submachine gun, though, the janitor could only exit on command, his broom abandoned, out the door and gone without a backward glance.

The manager had marked his office door with Chinese characters that probably meant Private or the rough equivalent. Ignoring it, the Executioner breezed in and caught a chunky, balding man behind the desk, with pound notes stacked in front of him.

"What's this, then?" With his eyes closed, Bolan could have easily mistaken this one for a native Briton.

"It's going-out-of-business time," Bolan stated. "You're about to have a fire sale."

"I don't understand."

"Let's put it this way," Bolan told him, palming an incendiary can and showing it to his reluctant host. "I'm burning this place down in sixty seconds. It's a little gift from me to Scarface Kam. You want to fry, by all means, stick around. If not..."

The manager was up and moving toward the door as Bolan stepped aside to let him pass. His running footsteps echoed in the hall outside, before the slamming back door cut them off. There were no soldiers in the club to challenge him, and that was fine with Bolan. It would make things easier.

White smoke was curling after the Executioner as he stepped into the alley and turned back toward his car. Before he tried another target on for size, he had to make a detour, touch base with a potential ally who had no idea who Bolan was or what he had in mind for London in the next few hours. It was a risk, admittedly, but if it worked, he would be miles ahead.

If not, well, he would worry over that when he had given it a shot. It wouldn't be the first time he had gambled, come up short and had to start from scratch.

As long as he was still alive, the battle would continue.

15

Ian Ward was sipping lukewarm coffee in a small café on Charing Cross, a few steps from the eastern edge of London's Chinatown, and wishing he could find another line of work. It was a thought that crossed his mind at least once every day, sometimes with greater frequency, and while he never acted on the notion, Ward believed that simply entertaining it was proof that he maintained some basic level of free will and independence from his job.

Or, maybe not.

Ward was an officer of the Special Branch of Scotland Yard. It used to be the Special *Irish* Branch, back in the good old days when Britain had only one group of terrorists to think about, but those days had evaporated long before Ward joined the force. While Special Branch still focused on political activities and crimes, its purview had expanded to include all kinds of terrorism, along with espionage, subversion and all manner of international crimes that had some kind of impact in Britain.

Ward's field of expertise, after a tour of military duty as a CID inspector in Hong Kong, was Chinese crime, political or otherwise. He knew the Triads well enough to have considered them a threat in London long before the brass at Scotland Yard shared his opinion. When they finally came around and recognized the Chinese role in crimes that ranged from drug dealing to importation of illegal aliens, the powers that be had shopped around for someone who could speak the language, both figuratively and literally, to spearhead law enforcement's counterattack. And they had been delighted, so they said, to find a man of Ian Ward's accomplishments already on the payroll.

Thus far, though, the great counteroffensive had been more of a waiting game, a process of observing and collecting information on the Triads, waiting for a chance to catch them dirty and achieve a major victory. It wasn't all surveillance, but the various arrests and criminal convictions had involved low-ranking members of the Chinese syndicate: the mules and runners, leg-breakers and front men for illegal gaming clubs. Wong Kam was still unscathed, still doing business at the same address, and from appearances, he had been branching out of late, abandoning his strictly mercenary line in favor of a fling at politics.

And not just any politics, at that. Your average mobster kept his hand in at the local level, bribing councillors and whatnot, but it was a rarity for criminals—the real professionals, at least—to dabble in the kind of revolutionary business that was normally reserved for diehard terrorists.

A rarity, but not unheard of.

Too bad, Ward considered, but he didn't speak the words aloud. It would look odd, to say the least, a copper talking to himself in a café like he was mental. Had he been at home, behind closed doors, it would have been a different story, but you always had to watch it in the public eye. Show no emotion on the job, espouse no principles beyond an abstract faith in justice and maintain the proper distance from those citizens who always needed your help but never really wanted to know you in real life.

He was about to flag down the teenaged waitress and ask her what in bloody hell was holding up his sandwich order, when a shadow fell across his table. Glancing up, Ward found himself confronted by a tall man, possibly American, well dressed . . . and armed. The bulge beneath his coat was subtle, but apparent to discriminating eyes.

Ward fought a brief, sharp rush of something close to panic. He had enemies, of course, but if the man had come to kill him, he would almost certainly be shooting now, instead of simply standing there like someone waiting for a bus.

Ward had thought the stranger was American, a snap judgment based upon his choice of clothes, and when he spoke the man removed all doubt.

"We need to have a talk," he said. "May I sit down?"

Ward thought about it for a moment and finally shrugged.

"Why not?"

THE LONG PALE SCAR on Wong Kam's face had been a gift from one of his competitors, back in the old days, when disputes were settled with an eye toward honor and finality. He had been ambushed on a Hong Kong street corner, his adversary coming at him with a dagger through the crowd of afternoon commuters. It was still a marvel to Wong Kam that the assassin, known for his prolific efforts and success in other cases, tried to stab him in the head, in lieu of ripping through his chest or abdomen, to pierce Kam's heart.

The end result was what he witnessed each and every morning in the bathroom mirror. Scarred, but still alive, he had been able to escape the scene before police arrived to question him, and he had spent the next eleven months pursuing his assailant, finishing the long hunt in Manila, mailing the assassin's head back to the man who had employed him in the first place.

Thus grew Kam's reputation as a man who always paid his debts, with interest due. So far, that reputation had been one of his more potent weapons in a world where enemies disguised themselves as friends and trust was a commodity more scarce than gold or platinum.

Kam disliked emotion, viewing any great display of sadness, love or anger as a sign of weakness. Still, his heart wasn't impervious to feeling, and the feeling that predominated at the moment was a crimson rage. Kam wished that he could scream and smash things, trash his office for a start, but that would only give his soldiers cause to doubt his sanity. Instead, he had to remain aloof, maintain control and plot the ruination of his enemies.

That Kam had enemies was never in dispute. A man didn't achieve the rank of red pole in the 14K without inflicting harm on others, and his victims—or, in many cases, their survivors—could be counted on to bear a grudge. Still, there was something in the latest incidents that elevated them above the normal scale of gang-related violence.

A round-eye meting out the damage, for example.

That was curious, and then some. It disturbed Kam and made him wonder if his treaties with the native thugs were on the point of breaking down.

Kam scowled and shook his head, as if responding to a spoken question. No, he thought, the locals would have been more subtle, maybe hired a Chinese crew to raid Ming's drugstore and the Shi-liu Club. Whoever was in fact responsible for those attacks wasn't afraid to show his round-eyed face on the streets of Chinatown.

And that required a certain nerve the local thugs hadn't possessed for years.

Outsiders, then, but knowing that didn't solve Kam's problem. He was still without a clue in terms of who to blame for the attacks, except that both of his surviving henchmen had agreed the shooter sounded more American than British.

Kam cursed and thumped the desktop with a pudgy fist. A damned American! He knew what that meant—what it could mean, anyway—with all the recent trouble in the States. Kam was busy with his deals in London, but he still had time to keep up with the flow of world events, especially as they affected his blood brothers overseas.

The Triad was a family, in much the same sense as the Mafia, although much older, steeped in the traditions of the East. A new recruit pledged life and limb to the protection of his Triad, in a ritual incorporating thirty-three specific promises, any one of which was violated on pain of hideous torture and death. In practice, though, the Triad's operation was distinctly regional, in spite of international connections that facilitated transportation of assorted contraband. Turmoil in New York, San Francisco or Vancouver might disturb Wong Kam, if friends of his were killed or injured, but it otherwise had no effect on daily life in London.

Not, that is, unless the man or men responsible should cross the broad Atlantic and attempt to play their childish tricks on Kam.

It wasn't Kam's place to insult the dead, but Sammy Ng and Vincent Liu had both been upstarts in the business, relatively young and inexperienced, despite their fearsome reputations. William Ma had been a veteran of brutal Tong wars, it was true, but Kam suspected that his old friend had been softened by the good life in New York. An enemy who thought the same of Scarface Kam would be mistaken, and it was the kind of error that would cost his life.

Kam liked his wine and women, to be sure, but he had never lost his fighting edge. The spirit that had saved him from that knife attack in Hong Kong lingered still, and he would slaughter anyone who tried to interfere with his established trade in London.

It might even be a pleasure, he decided, looking forward to the old, familiar taste of blood.

BOLAN HAD ALREADY SETTLED in a chair across from Ian Ward, when the policeman said, "By all means, have a seat. And may I buy your lunch, as well?"

The heavy note of sarcasm made Bolan smile. "No thanks," he said. "I'm fine."

"Who are you, by the way?"

"Mike Blanski."

Bolan flashed a laminated ID card that named him as an agent of the CIA. It was the real thing, more or less, except for Bolan's name, a prop obtained "through channels" with some help from Stony Man.

"Should I be flattered or defensive?" Ward inquired. "I mean, it isn't every day the Company takes notice of a lowly copper like myself."

"You're much too modest," Bolan said.

"Not half. What is it that you want?"

"Some information ought to do the trick."

The waitress came with Ward's lunch, the Special Branch man letting her retreat before he spoke again.

"What kind of information did you have in mind?"

"I'm working on the Triad beat," Bolan replied. "More specifically, Triad connections with the mainland government that have facilitated trade in contraband and possible subversive actions."

"Ah, the Yellow Peril rides again."

"You never know."

"From what I hear," Ward said, "the 14K is self-destructing in the States these days."

"You keep yourself informed."

"I'd be bloody useless otherwise," Ward told him. "Would your visit to our city be connected to the events in San Francisco and New York, by any chance?"

"Could be."

"Are you aware we've had two incidents ourselves? This very morning, as it happens. A coincidence, perhaps."

"You never know."

"How is it that Americans appear so fond of playing ignorant?" Ward asked. "If you must know, it's not your most attractive feature."

"It cuts down on explanations, I suppose."

"You've come to me, I must assume, because you're worried that the brass at Special Branch would brush you off. That means you either think I'm dumb enough to risk my job on your behalf, or you have something sweet to offer me as a reward, if I cooperate."

"I'd say you're definitely not a stupid man."

"Right. Let's get down to business then. What is it that you want from me, and what's the trade-off?"

"In the States, we managed to identify a ChiCom agent who was working closely with the 14K. His name was Luk Pang, a black ops specialist they shipped in from the mainland."

"And?"

"He had a fatal accident last night, but we assume Pang has a counterpart in Europe, possibly in London. If he's not based here, the man I'm looking for would certainly touch base from time to time with Scarface Kam."

"You know our red pole?"

"By reputation only," Bolan said. "We may meet later, if I'm lucky."

"That depends upon your definition of good luck, I'd say."

"Right now, I'm more concerned about Kam's contact with Beijing. The smuggling would be someone else's problem, down the line."

"Two questions come to mind," Ward said. "First off, what happens to this fellow, if and when you find him. Secondly, what's in it for my service if you should receive assistance in your hunt?"

"You want straight answers, I assume?"

"That's always best."

"All right. Let's say I'm thinning out the herd. The State Department can't negotiate a deal like this, and Congress would go crazy if they knew about it. Get the tabloid press involved, and you'd have open calls for war. Forget about whatever trade agreements and negotiations on the human rights agenda may be in the pipeline. Sometimes surgical removal is the best—the only—option. Sad, but true.''

"Assuming for the sake of argument that I agree with you, there's still the matter of my second question."

"The benefit to you would be immediate disruption of whatever plans the 14K and Beijing had in mind for the United Kingdom. On the side, I would anticipate at least a partial breakdown in the local Triad's operation. If you don't mind batting cleanup, you could bag a few of the survivors when the smoke clears."

"So, you're asking for a hunting license?"

Bolan frowned and shook his head. "I'd settle for a name."

"You've placed me in a most precarious position, Mr. Blanski. Here you are, effectively confessing your intent to murder one or more specific individuals in London. By all rights, I should arrest you on the spot."

"Unless you're wired," Bolan said, "it would never stick."

"But the embarrassment might slow you down."

"Your call, of course."

"Conversely, if we never had this conversation, then I've no grounds for arresting anyone, or filing a report with my superiors on ugly rumors that I've never heard."

"That's very true."

"It would be absolutely inappropriate for me to help you, Mr. Blanski."

"As I said, your call."

"The last thing I would ever do is name a well-regarded Chinese businessman like Tu Sheng as a suspected agent of the Beijing government, involved in scheming with the Triads."

Bolan filed the name away and said, "I never heard of him."

"Exactly. And I certainly wouldn't inform a stranger that this suspect had a flat just off Gerrard Street, two blocks east of St. John's Hospital."

"I understand."

"Besides, if I was unprofessional enough to give that information out, I'd jeopardize the team of Chinese officers we have on round-the-clock surveillance of the subject."

"And we can't have that."

"By no means." Ward glanced at his watch. "I really must be getting back to work now, Mr. Blanski. If you ever find yourself in London, look me up."

With that, Ward rose and left the table, sticking Bolan with the check. It came to £5.95. The soldier left a ten-pound note to cover it and gave Ward a chance to clear the restaurant and get a fair head start before he followed the policeman out.

So far, so good.

Now all he had to do was twist the Chinese dragon's tail enough to make it scream, while trying not to let himself get fried or stepped on in the process.

THE FIRST ALARM came in at 3:19 p.m., a round-eye shooting up the Dou-yar Club on Newport Place. Chin Lee and his three gunmen were patrolling in the area, perhaps two blocks away, when they were notified by radio. With any luck, police wouldn't arrive before they had a chance to run the white man down and finish him.

Lee hoped so, anyway.

It could only help his reputation as a soldier if he caught the man who had been giving Scarface Kam such fits all day. This made the third or fourth attack in Chinatown within as many hours, and Lee knew it had to be some kind of crazy man. Who else would dare to bring down the Triad's wrath on himself in such a manner, knowing it would cost his life?

Lee's orders were to take the man alive, if possible, and bring him in for questioning, but from the tone in which those orders were delivered, he understood that he wouldn't be punished if the round-eye suffered fatal injuries. All unavoidable, of course, while putting up resistance in the street.

Dead men were much easier to handle, and Lee saw no reason why his own life should be placed in jeopardy to save a man whose fate was sealed, no matter what. The round-eye would be killed regardless, whether Kam had time to question him or not, and the result would be the same. His death would send a message back to any friends or allies he might have, assuming there was more to the attacks than just some maniac at large.

Two minutes brought them to the Dou-yar Club, and they were just in time to see the round-eye coming out. He turned to lob some object through the open doorway, then turned to his right along the sidewalk, striding swiftly toward a dark blue Saab 9000 parked a few doors down the street.

"Get after him!" Lee snapped.

The car surged forward as Lee thumbed the safety off his compact Sterling Mk 4 submachine gun. In the back seat, he could hear his soldiers readying their weapons, while he concentrated on the target just ahead.

The round-eye heard them, maybe felt them coming, for he bolted, sprinting to the Saab without a backward glance. He had some kind of instincts, that one, but there was still a chance for them to box him at the curb and finish it right there.

"Quickly! Don't let him—"

They were already too late. Lee cursed and slapped his driver as the Saab roared into motion, threatening to leave them in its dust. Lee imagined he could hear the round-eye laughing at him.

"Catch him if you want to live, goddamn—"

The Dou-yar Club exploded, spewing fire and smoking trash into the street. Lee's driver swung wide to avoid the worst of it, but a smoking shoe came down in front of them, clung briefly to the hood of their car before it slid away.

"After him!"

Lee punctuated the command with a jab of his weapon to the driver's ribs. Another burst of speed, and they were gaining on the Swedish sports car now, too slowly for Lee's taste, but gaining all the same.

Lee rolled down his window and prepared to start shooting when he had a decent target. Any moment now the round-eye would be close enough for him to cut loose with the Sterling, spray the Saab with copper-jacketed 9 mm rounds. He might not hit the driver, but the car was something else. It would be difficult to miss—tires, gas tank, windows, all of it. And once they stopped the car...

At first Lee didn't understand what he was seeing. Was the round-eye signaling a turn in the old-fashioned way, his right arm sticking out the window? No, wait, there was something in his hand, dark, egg-shaped, bouncing on the pavement when he dropped it, wobbling right in front of Chin Lee's car.

"Watch out!"

The warning came too late to save them. The grenade exploded with a flash, and Lee felt his car begin to swerve, the stupid driver throwing up both hands to shield his face from the explosion. Lee reached out to grab the wheel, but shrapnel from the blast had shredded one—or maybe both—of his front tires. The vehicle didn't respond, continuing to swerve. They crashed into a minivan parked at the curb, and Lee smacked his forehead on the doorpost, felt the Sterling bruise his shin as it slid down between his knees onto the floor.

He started snapping orders, didn't ask the others if they were all right. Whatever petty injuries they might have suffered in the crash would have to wait. Their weapons were enough to earn them jail time, but the worst of it wouldn't be facing prosecution in the white man's court.

The worst of it would be explaining abject failure to Wong Kam, the more so if they shamed the family by letting the police arrest them.

"Hurry! We must go!"

Lee tucked the Sterling awkwardly inside his jacket as he scrambled from the car. A shattered radiator spilled its contents on the pavement. He could hear the engine ticking as it cooled.

Lee ducked into the nearest alley, heard the others close behind him, running to catch up. With any luck they could avoid the officers who took the call, and Kam's people could report the vehicle as stolen. After that, the only thing Lee had to think about was saving face when he reported abject failure to his master.

Kam wouldn't be amused.

Lee decided that to save himself, his men, he would be forced to lie more eloquently than he ever had before.

A FLAT JUST OFF Gerrard Street, two blocks east of St. John's Hospital. He had no way of knowing if his target was at home this evening, but the Executioner was bound to check and see.

It had been touch and go there for a moment, with the flying squad of Triad soldiers, but Kam's troops were used to having things their own way on the streets of Chinatown. With arrogance to spare, it never seriously crossed their minds that anyone—much less a white man—could defeat them on their own home turf. They would be learning, slowly, but the habits of a lifetime could be difficult to break. For Bolan's part, he counted on the overconfidence of enemies to help his cause.

The ChiCom agent, Tu Sheng, for instance, was a man who held himself aloof from the daily operations of his allies in the 14K. He would be conscious of the recent raids in Chinatown, perhaps informed of Luk Pang's demise in the

United States, but Bolan hoped he wouldn't run. Not yet. He wanted one clean shot, one chance to get it right and break the next link in the chain. That done, he could dismantle Kam's fat operation at his leisure.

Bolan found the old apartment house, parked two doors down and walked in through the front as if he lived there. Considerable money had been spent inside to modernize the place, while still maintaining the distinctive Chinese atmosphere. Wallpaper in the lobby, artwork, everything had been coordinated to remind the tenants and their visitors of life back home—a home that some of them, at least, had never seen.

Tu Sheng had seen the mainland, though, and not so long ago. A hasty background check through Stony Man identified the target as a veteran player in the Chinese cloak-and-dagger game. Now forty-six, he had been traveling through Western Europe for the past three years, ostensibly on business that would help Beijing to "Westernize" and leave some portions of the Maoist past behind. In fact, Sheng had closed million-dollar deals in rice, petroleum and rubber, but it was his leisure-time activities that interested the Executioner.

Throughout his European travels, Tu Sheng had been in touch with terrorists of left and right, along with ranking leaders of the Triads and at least one elder statesman of the Mafia, in Sicily. It added up to trouble, with the details still a trifle vague. Whatever Sheng was up to, Bolan meant to close his show without delay.

He passed by the elevator and took the stairs, eight flights to put him out on four. There was a sleepy-looking guard on Tu Sheng's door, relaxing in a folding chair, some kind of skin magazine open on his lap. The soldier glanced up, tried to scramble at the sight of Bolan's automatic, with the silencer attached, and lost it as his chair collapsed beneath him, pinning him like some demented Venus flytrap.

Bolan shot him once to keep him down, and used his forward motion to add weight behind the kick that snapped Sheng's lock. He barged across the threshold, caught another Chinese gunner just vaulting off the couch and shot him in the face.

Two down, and number three was just emerging from the kitchen with some kind of sandwich in his hand. He dropped it on the carpet, reaching for the handgun tucked into his belt, but Bolan had his target locked by then, a parabellum mangler ripping through the gunman's chest to drop him in his tracks.

He stepped around the dead man, moving toward the master bedroom. There, he found the walk-in closet standing open, empty hangers and the blank spots in a shoe rack telling him that Sheng had packed sufficient clothes to stay away from home for at least several days. If he was running, Bolan would assume the ChiCom agent could acquire whatever else he needed when he found another place to hide. The three dead soldiers would have been assigned to watch the flat, perhaps maintain the fiction that their master was at home, to see if anyone came calling in his absence.

Damn! Another miss.

Which meant that he would have to fall back on Plan B, go after Kam and hope to catch the two of them together. It had worked on Staten Island, but he knew it might be pressing things to count on getting lucky twice in two days' time.

Whatever, he could only take the shot and see what happened. The alternative was backing off, losing momentum, while his enemies worked overtime to patch up their defenses.

That was unacceptable to Bolan, one short step from an admission of defeat. And he wasn't defeated yet, by any means. If Tu Sheng evaded him today, he would resume the hunt tomorrow, call for help from Stony Man if necessary, anything to see the job completed.

First things first.

Wong Kam had an appointment with the Executioner, and Bolan didn't mean to keep him waiting any longer.

16

Like many of his Triad counterparts in other Western cities, Wong Kam had a home away from home, outside of Chinatown. It wasn't far away, roughly seven hundred meters as the crow flew, from the Chinese enclave to a stylish house on Adams Street, near the Victoria Embankment Gardens, fronting on the Thames. Still, time and space were relative, and Wong Kam's hideaway could just as well have been light years from Chinatown, considering the pale complexion of the neighborhood.

A drive-by showed him that the wrought iron gates were closed on Kam's driveway, but the Executioner got lucky four doors down, with the discovery of a deserted house. He didn't know or care exactly where the tenants were, or when they were expected to return. The carport hid his Saab from prying eyes, and Bolan had no need to go inside the house. In shadow, he removed his street clothes to reveal the blacksuit underneath, slipped on his military webbing and removed his weapons from the trunk. A bandolier of extra magazines for the IW assault rifle was slung across his chest, and Bolan's pistol belt was heavy with grenades. Whatever waited for him in the house of Scarface Kam, he had done everything within his power to be prepared.

The street would be too risky, Bolan knew, and so he traveled through the backyards of the homes that separated him from Kam's estate.

He reached the fence that separated Kam from his nearest neighbor, pausing long enough to scan the spacious yard and check for sentries. One man lounged by the swimming pool, another sat at the back door of the house, but neither one paid much attention to his job.

So far, so good.

A creeping shadow, Bolan slipped across the fence and landed on the soft grass in a crouch.

THE FIRST ROUND from the silenced Browning caught the sentry by the swimming pool as he was turning, reaching underneath his coat for something. Impact threw the human target backward, and he landed in the deep end with a splash.

The second guard was up and moving now, already reaching for his weapon, opening his mouth to raise a general alarm. It was a risky shot, but Bolan had no choice. He swung around, made target acquisition from a range of forty feet and stroked the trigger twice. Round one went between the Triad gunner's open lips, while number two bored underneath his chin and bottled up his larynx.

Time was the crucial factor now, and Bolan understood that there was none to spare. He had to get inside the house, find Scarface Kam and see if Tu Sheng had run to Kam for sanctuary in his darkest hour.

The door swung open just as Bolan got there to reveal a pair of young Chinese. For all he knew, it was the changing of the guard, but the Executioner didn't care. He had to dump these gunners now, before he could get on about his business with their master.

Bolan had the Browning automatic in his hand, prepared to mete out silent death. There was no hesitation as he raised the pistol, fired a parabellum mangler through the first soldier's face at something close to skin-touch range. Behind him, number two was quick enough to get out his side arm and thumb the hammer back before a bullet found him, ripping through his chest. He triggered three quick rounds as he was falling, bullets snapping through the air a foot or so to Bolan's left.

It didn't matter that they missed. The shots were loud enough to rouse the house, if not the dead, and Bolan knew he would be facing opposition from that point on. He tucked the Browning back inside its holster, slipped the short IW off his shoulder and kept on moving, ready for the worst that Scarface Kam could throw at him.

He cleared the pantry, then the kitchen proper, meeting his first real opposition in the formal dining room—three soldiers, two of them with stubby riot shotguns pointed at the door where Bolan stood. Raw instinct saved him, as he threw himself facedown on thick shag carpeting, the dining table and its chairs obscuring his adversaries' field of fire.

They cut loose anyway, buckshot demolishing a couple of the oaken chairs, reducing them to splintered kindling. Bolan wriggled underneath the table, sighting on three pairs of legs that were his only clear view of the enemy. The IW was set for full-auto fire, and he burned up one-third of its 30-round mag in one burst, tracking from left to right, aiming for ankles and shins.

His opposition gave up shouting curses and started to scream as the 5.56 mm tumblers ripped into their legs below the knees. Two of them fell together, like exhausted ballroom dancers slumping in a clinch, and Bolan nailed them with a second burst that shattered two skulls for the price of one. The third man sprawled away from his companions, lost his shotgun as he fell and started to scrabble after it with wheezing grunts of pain. A 3-round burst from Bolan's rifle flipped him over on his back and pinned him there, his body twitching slightly as the life ran out of him through ragged blowholes in his torso.

The Executioner vaulted to his feet, ignoring the bloody corpses as he stepped around them, and looked for his next live enemy. It wouldn't take him long to find another adversary, he imagined, but the men he wanted most were still eluding him.

Wong Kam.

Tu Sheng.

The Executioner was on a hunting expedition, and he wouldn't stop until he found his prey.

WONG KAM WAS TREMBLING as he slid the hidden cabinet open, lifting out the Chinese copy of a Russian AK-47 that had been a gift from Tu Sheng on Kam's last birthday. He hadn't fired the weapon since that weekend, on a boozy outing in the country, but he knew exactly how it worked, what it could do. Possession of such rifles was forbidden under British law, but that was certainly the least of Kam's criminal offenses. The police knew nothing of his little toy, and if they did find out, Kam was confident that well-placed bribes could make the trouble go away.

Unlike the sounds of mortal combat emanating from downstairs.

Kam's unknown enemies had forced their way into his very home, an insult that could only be repaid in blood. He snapped an order at the two young soldiers who stood watching him, and they retreated from his private study, rushing off to join their comrades in the fight that had been joined below.

Kam had a dozen soldiers covering his home, the most that he felt he could spare from Chinatown under the circumstances. Now he wished for more, but even if he called for reinforcements, they wouldn't arrive in time. One of his round-eyed neighbors would be on the telephone to Scotland Yard by now, and that might very well turn out to be a blessing in disguise. Kam normally preferred to shun police, except when he was paying off some ranking member of the force, but he could use some help this night. If there were questions, afterward—about his men or their weapons—Kam would use his cash and influence to smooth things over at the top.

It was the way a businessman did business in the modern world, and Kam had always been the very model of propriety in London.

He could also be a ruthless killer, when it was called for. As it was tonight.

A double shot of vodka, for the extra courage it would give him, and the red pole left his study, hesitating for a moment in the upstairs hallway as he listened to the sharp, staccato sounds of gunfire from below. It was impossible to say which guns were his and which belonged to his opponents, but the question would soon be resolved.

Kam started toward the staircase, walking with the rifle braced against his hip, the safety off, his index finger curled around the trigger. Anyone who threatened the red pole in his own home was a dead man. He would spill that person's blood himself, and thus set an example for his men.

What better way to guarantee a bond of fear and ultimate respect?

He smelled cordite, a treasured fragrance that was mostly lacking from his life since Kam was elevated to the role of an executive. He delegated dirty work these days, but something told him it was time for more direct involvement in the daily problems of his family. No one could fault him if he chose to lead his soldiers by example, rather than directing them from a position on the sidelines. It was perfectly all right, as long as Kam took care to guard his back and gave police no cause to issue warrants in his name.

The sudden shock of an explosion rippled through the floor beneath his feet. Kam felt it, even with the thick carpet underfoot. It hadn't been powerful enough for plastique. Some kind of hand grenade, perhaps, or even a small charge of gelignite.

Downstairs, a number of the guns were silenced in the aftermath of the explosion. Kam didn't like the implications of that, since he knew his soldiers weren't equipped with hand grenades. If anyone had suffered from the blast, his men were the most likely victims. That, in turn, meant his defenses had been whittled down, increasing danger to himself.

Determined to survive and prove himself a leader, Wong Kam swallowed bitter fear and kept moving toward the stairs.

THEY HAD BEEN WAITING for him in the spacious living room, two soldiers crouched behind a sofa, one more burrowed in behind a fat recliner, none of them inclined to take a chance and show himself before the enemy had been exposed. At sight of Bolan coming though the doorway, all three opened up at once, their submachine guns chewing wallpaper to tattered ribbons, gouging divots in the wall and raining plaster dust.

The easy chair that sheltered Bolan was constructed out of heavy wood and supple leather dyed maroon to match the great room's color scheme. It stopped the first few bullets well enough, but Bolan knew his cover wouldn't stand up to the concentrated fire of three guns, much less the support troops who were surely on their way by now. He had to move, and soon, or they would nail him down and finish him.

He palmed a frag grenade, released the safety pin and lobbed the bomb overhand in the direction of the couch. The pitch was short, but he got lucky, saw the lethal egg bounce once on sofa cushions and drop out of sight behind the couch. One of the hidden gunners screamed, but it was already too late for raising the alarm.

The blast made Bolan's ears ring, but he followed up instinctively, burst out from cover while the shrapnel was still flying, smacking into walls and ceiling. Writing off the two men who had crouched behind the sofa, Bolan turned his piece on the recliner, braced and ready as the third man stuck his head up for a peek—and lost it to a burst from Bolan's automatic rifle, fired with almost surgical precision at a range of twenty feet. The dead man slumped back out of sight, and the warrior was about to check his comrades when another pair of weapons cut loose on him from the stairs.

He swiveled, firing as he dropped back under cover, and saw a pair of gunmen on the staircase, armed with compact SMGs. Their aim was spoiled by haste, fear and anger, but it wouldn't take them long to get a grip and start to put their rounds on target. With mobility and altitude, they could defeat his cover, flush him out or kill him where he sat with interlocking streams of fire.

And that meant Bolan had to take them now, before they overcame that first, confused reaction and began to think like soldiers, act as a team.

He swallowed hard and came up firing in the face of blazing guns. His first rounds caught the shooter on his left, the lower of the two on the staircase, gutting him and spinning him around. Before his body hit the landing, Bolan was already targeting the other Triad gunman, emptying his rifle's magazine in one long burst that raked the stairs and found his human target trying to retreat, with nowhere safe to hide.

He watched the dead man stagger, legs turned into rubber by the magic of a bullet through the heart. His lifeless adversary tumbled headlong down the stairs to join his sidekick in a heap at Bolan's level, tangled arms and legs smeared with blood.

He was reloading when a sudden movement flickered at the corner of his eye. A solitary figure glared at Bolan from the head of the staircase, cradling a Kalashnikov, with one hand wrapped around the weapon's pistol grip. The long scar down one cheek told Bolan he was looking at Wong Kam.

Their guns went off together, hammering the parlor's smoky atmosphere. The AK's bullets raked a coffee table off to Bolan's right and shredded several magazines, then marched across the carpet, getting closer by the heartbeat, ripping through the carpet pad to find wood underneath. Another second would have done it, but the IW was locked on target, spitting death in rapid fire, and Kam staggered, lurching backward, crimson geysers spattering the wall behind him as he dropped his weapon, crumpled, fell.

It seemed to take forever, racing up the stairs, but Bolan made the trip in seconds flat, eyes sweeping back and forth between the upstairs landing and the ground floor, ready to react if any other gunmen showed themselves. When none appeared, he let himself relax a little, crouched beside Wong Kam and found that he was breathing.

Barely.

"Tu Sheng," Bolan said, grabbing Scarface by the hair and wobbling his head from side to side. "Where is he?"

Glassy eyes tried focusing on Bolan's face, but quickly gave it up. Kam tried to speak, blew scarlet bubbles in the place of words and died with Bolan's fingers tangled in his hair.

How long before the cops arrived?

He searched the second floor in record time, found no one hiding in the study, in the bedrooms, in the closets.

Zip.

Tu Sheng was nowhere to be found.

Downstairs again, he heard the first faint echoes of police sirens. They would be turning onto Adams Street in moments, boxing him. He had to leave without delay, if he was going to continue tracking Tu Sheng.

And there was never any question that he would continue, press the hunt until he found his man, and on beyond that point, to find Sheng's masters.

Call his London blitz the end of the beginning, then, and push on through the darkness, searching for a ray of light.

He passed more corpses in the dining room, the kitchen, in the yard outside. The sirens had drawn closer as he scaled the fence, lights winking on in homes to either side of Scarface Kam's.

Too late.

The Executioner was out of there. He didn't know exactly where the hunt would take him, but he had a fair idea of where to start.

The trail was fresh, and he was on his way.

God help whoever tried to hold him back.

* * * * * *

The heart-stopping action continues in the second book of The Red Dragon Trilogy: Steel Claws, *coming in July.*

**A mutating killer virus becomes
a terrorist's ticket to power**

STONY MAN™ 23
The Perishing Game

A mysterious virus has annihilated two towns, fueling dread that these were test sites for the most insidious form of terrorism—a killer virus, genetically engineered and racially selective. When the mutant virus turns into an equal-opportunity destroyer, capable of killing diverse populations, the Stony Man commandos are the only thing standing between a megalomaniac and mass extinction.

Take
4 explosive books
plus a
mystery bonus
FREE

Mail to: Gold Eagle Reader Service
3010 Walden Ave.
P.O. Box 1394
Buffalo, NY 14240-1394

YEAH! Rush me 4 FREE Gold Eagle novels and my FREE mystery gift.
Then send me 4 brand-new novels every other month as they come off
the presses. Bill me at the low price of just $14.80* for each shipment—
a saving of 12% off the cover prices for all four books! There is NO extra
charge for postage and handling! There is no minimum number of books I
must buy. I can always cancel at any time simply by returning a shipment
at your cost or by returning any shipping statement marked "cancel." Even
if I never buy another book from Gold Eagle, the 4 free books and surprise
gift are mine to keep forever.

164 BPM ANQY

Name	(PLEASE PRINT)	
Address		Apt. No.
City	State	Zip

Signature (if under 18, parent or guardian must sign)

* Terms and prices subject to change without notice. Sales tax applicable in
NY. This offer is limited to one order per household and not valid to
present subscribers. Offer not available in Canada.

AC-94

**American hostages abroad have
one chance of getting out alive**

BLACK OPS #3

DEEP TERROR

created by MICHAEL KASNER

Americans are increasingly in danger, at home and abroad. Created
by an elite cadre of red-tape-cutting government officials, the
Black Ops commandos exist to avenge such acts of terror.

Don't miss the last book of this miniseries, available in August
at your favorite retail outlet.

**Don't miss out on the action in these titles featuring
THE EXECUTIONER®, ABLE TEAM® and PHOENIX FORCE®!**

The Arms Trilogy

The Executioner #61195	SELECT FIRE	$3.50 U.S. $3.99 CAN.	☐ ☐
The Executioner #61196	TRIBURST	$3.50 U.S. $3.99 CAN.	☐ ☐
The Executioner #61197	ARMED FORCE	$3.50 U.S. $3.99 CAN.	☐ ☐

The Executioner®

#64204	RESCUE RUN	$3.50 U.S. $3.99 CAN.	☐ ☐
#64205	HELL ROAD	$3.50 U.S. $3.99 CAN.	☐ ☐
#64206	HUNTING CRY	$3.75 U.S. $4.25 CAN.	☐ ☐
#64207	FREEDOM STRIKE	$3.75 U.S. $4.25 CAN.	☐ ☐
#64208	DEATH WHISPER	$3.75 U.S. $4.25 CAN.	☐ ☐
#64209	ASIAN CRUCIBLE	$3.75 U.S. $4.25 CAN.	☐ ☐

(limited quantities available on certain titles)

TOTAL AMOUNT	$
POSTAGE & HANDLING	$
($1.00 for one book, 50¢ for each additional)	
APPLICABLE TAXES*	$_____
TOTAL PAYABLE	$_____
(check or money order—please do not send cash)	

To order, complete this form and send it, along with a check or money order for the total above, payable to Gold Eagle Books, to: **In the U.S.:** 3010 Walden Avenue, P.O. Box 9077, Buffalo, NY 14269-9077; **In Canada:** P.O. Box 636, Fort Erie, Ontario, L2A 5X3.

Name:_____

Address:_____ City:_____

State/Prov.:_____ Zip/Postal Code:_____

*New York residents remit applicable sales taxes.
  Canadian residents remit applicable GST and provincial taxes.

GEBACK14